I0838527

DREAMS OF THE DAMNED

ATLANTIS LEGACY, BOOK 3

LINDSEY SPARKS   WRITING AS   LINDSEY FAIRLEIGH

RUBUS PRESS

Copyright © 2020 by Rubus Press
All rights reserved.

This book is a work of fiction. All characters, organizations, and events are products of the author's imaginations or are used fictitiously. No reference to any real person, living or dead, is intended or should be inferred.

Editing by Fresh as a Daisy Editing
www.freshasadaisyediting.com

Cover by We Got You Covered
www.wegotyoucoveredbookdesign.com

ISBN: 9781949485172

MORE BOOK BY LINDSEY SPARKS

ECHO TRILOGY

Echo in Time

Resonance

Time Anomaly

Dissonance

Ricochet Through Time

KAT DUBOIS CHRONICLES

Ink Witch

Outcast

Underground

Soul Eater

Judgement

Afterlife

ATLANTIS LEGACY

Sacrifice of the Sinners

Legacy of the Lost

Fate of the Fallen

Dreams of the Damned

Song of the Soulless

Blood of the Broken

Rise of the Revenants

ALLWORLD ONLINE

AO: Pride & Prejudice

AO: The Wonderful Wizard of Oz

Vertigo

THE ENDING SERIES

The Ending Beginnings: Omnibus Edition

After The Ending

Into The Fire

Out Of The Ashes

Before The Dawn

World Before

THE ENDING LEGACY

World After

For more information on Lindsey and her books:

www.authorlindseysparks.com

Join Lindsey's mailing list to stay up to date on releases

AND to get a FREE copy of *Sacrifice of the Sinners*.

www.authorlindseysparks.com/sacrifice

To read Lindsey's books as she writes them, check her out on Patreon:

https://www.patreon.com/lindseysparks

ACKNOWLEDGMENTS

Thank you so much to my Patreon Patrons, who support my work on a monthly basis:

Olivia Rodriguez
Carlotta Woolcock
Teri Lindley
Fred Oelrich
Aisling Ó Béara
Allison Mayer
Stephanie Oaks

[1]

"Agh!" I cried out as a well-placed kick to the sternum sent me stumbling backward. The heel of my boot caught on an ancient paving stone, and I rolled, ass over teakettle, hissing curses along the way. I landed ungracefully on my hands and knees and spat out a mouthful of sand.

A shadow blocked the moonlight, and heaving a breath, I raised my head to take in my attacker. Meg stood with her fists on her hips and a suppressed smile tugging at her lips. Behind her, the clear night sky formed a starry backdrop above the outlines of the two largest of the famed pyramids of Giza—those belonging to Khufu and Khafre—and a halo of silver moonlight surrounded the upper half of her body. The channels running the length of her form-fitting hoplon suit glowed a subtle amber, matching the stone in her activated regulator, signaling that her psychic powers were suppressed.

Her smug expression set my teeth on edge, and I growled low in my throat. Before Meg could get too comfortable in her victory, I dove for her legs, wrapping my arms around her thighs and knocking her onto her back.

Meg grunted with the impact, and sand went flying all

around us. Lips twisting into something that was part grimace, part grin—and pure aggression—she gripped my braid and yanked my head to the side.

I yelped, gritting my teeth and arching my neck to alleviate the sharp pain in my scalp.

Meg used the shock from the dirty hair-pull maneuver to snake her legs around my neck in a brutal choke hold. Her thighs were a steel vice cutting off my air supply, and a whole new set of stars danced around the edge of my vision as my blood ran dangerously low on oxygen. I clawed at her legs, trying to dig my fingers in between her thighs and my throat, but it was no use. She was too strong.

I double tapped the outside of Meg's thigh, letting her know I was giving up. For the third time in a row.

Here I was—Persephone, a psychic Olympian warrior of the Order of Amazons with seventeen lifetime's worth of combat training and experience, and I couldn't even beat a seventeen-year-old girl. Sure, she was also a psychic warrior—though a human one—born and raised in a hidden underground city buried deep within the heart of the Amazon Rainforest, but she was still a relative child. Besting her shouldn't have been a struggle. It should have been a given. But it wasn't because I wasn't just Peri. I was also *Cora*, a twenty-six-year-old gamer who had clocked thousands of combat hours in the virtual world, but about twelve in the real world.

Meg's legs relaxed, and I sucked in a much-needed breath and flopped onto my back on the sand. I stared up at the night sky, watching as the darkness of impending unconsciousness receded from the edges of my vision with each cherished breath and the stars flared to their full glory overhead.

"Let's take a break," Meg said from beside me. A sidelong glance told me she wasn't in *much* better shape than me, sprawled on her back on the sand, breathing hard. Beating me hadn't been easy for her. So, at least there was that.

But I knew she had only suggested taking a break because she could sense my irritation at being bested by her—again—through the psychic bond we had forged barely a week ago when she had pledged her life to mine in recompense for attempting to kidnap me. No matter how tightly we squeezed the psychic vice to tamp down on the bond, we hadn't figured out a way to block it completely. A little bit always trickled through. Enough that I could sense Meg's train of thought before she even opened her mouth.

"You'll get stronger, Cora. And your stamina has already increased." As she spoke, her compassion and understanding for my situation trickled through our bond, and I smashed my lips together to keep myself from lashing out at her. Anger roiled in my belly, but none of it was aimed at her. "It just takes time," she added weakly.

I growled in frustration and rolled onto my hands and knees, then climbed to my feet, brushing my hands off on my outer thighs. Meg sat up, reclining back on her hands.

I despised being so weak. Never—*never*—in any of my lives had I felt so pathetic or helpless. Four days ago, my two selves had become one. I was no longer just Cora, the reclusive gamer *or* just Peri, the psychic warrior—I was both Cora *and* Peri, and I had all the knowledge and skills I had acquired over my many lifetimes. In theory, at least.

In the case of physical combat, my brain knew what my body needed to do, but my body was lagging, unable to execute moves I'd done a thousand times before. And the worst part of it was that this was my own fault. Two decades of playing video games had done little to prepare my body for anything beyond sitting for long periods of time. Even if I hadn't known who—or *what*—I really was, it was no excuse for the extreme neglect I'd shown toward my own body. I was mad at my mom and Emi for letting me embrace such a sedentary, slothful lifestyle, but I was mostly mad at myself for letting my apparently intrinsic lazy nature mold me into such a worthless piece of—

"Wow," Meg said dryly, drawing my attention down to her. "And I thought I was the queen of self-loathing." She stood, brushed off her backside, and bowed to me with a dramatic flourish. "I stand corrected, your highness."

I stared at her, unamused.

At the crunch of sand grinding against stone, we both turned to watch Raiden make his way up the ancient limestone walkway cutting through the desert sand, leading from the Great Sphinx to our favored sparring location behind the massive monument. He raised a hand to wave, his full lips spreading into a hesitant smile.

I sighed, tension seeping into my shoulders.

Raiden was the last person I wanted to see right now. He was a glaring reminder of just how weak I had been. Of just how much I had needed him to help me rescue my mom and track down Hades. Me, a psychic warrior of the Order of Amazons, relying on a *man* to complete a mission. Olympian men couldn't even become Amazons; only the females of our species were capable of withstanding the genetic modification that enabled our psychic gifts. We were the top of the food chain in Olympian society, the best of the best. It was unheard of for one of my kind to take the backseat to anyone other than another Amazon warrior. But with Raiden, I had been the follower, the sidekick, the backup for pretty much my whole life. The memory of how much I had relied on him—of how much I had truly needed his help—disgusted me.

And yet, I loved Raiden with all my heart. Or, at least, with the Cora half of my heart. Now that Hades was awake, my love life was a lot more complicated.

But the more time I spent as my true self, aware of all I had experienced over my many lifetimes—both as Peri *and* as Cora —the harder it was to reconcile myself with whom I had become in *this* life. How was it that this version of me had turned out so differently from all the others? Did my training truly make up that much of who I was—who I had been? Did my life as Cora represent my true nature, or was she—I—just another product of my environment? To say I was having an identity crisis would be a gross understatement. I felt like I was losing my damn mind.

"Mind if I join you?" Raiden asked as he veered off the path and trudged through the sand toward us. "Don't want to get too out of shape…"

I gritted my teeth, practically grinding them together. Raiden looked like an action figure turned to flesh and bone, his body honed to combat perfection after nearly a decade spent in the military. The idea that he was on his way to *getting out of shape* was beyond laughable.

I hadn't grappled with Raiden since that night in the hotel in Rome when I had awakened him from a nightmare, and his half-asleep self had attempted to strangle the life out of me. I'd beaten him then, but with the way my arm muscles currently trembled with fatigue, there was no doubt the outcome of a match between us now would be dismal—for me. I couldn't handle losing to him right now. I was too deeply entrenched in my latest identity crisis.

Planting my hands on my hips, I stared off at the top half of the pyramid of Khafre, all that was visible of the landmark over the sloping sand. "You two go ahead," I said, my voice distant as my thoughts wandered to other ways to improve my physical fitness. My abysmal stamina was my weakest point and putting in more effort in that department would go a long way toward reclaiming my former glory.

My eyes narrowed on the top of the pyramid. It was maybe a quarter of a mile away. Sprinting there and back a few times every day ought to do the trick. My stamina would be up to snuff in no time.

I started toward the pyramid at a jog. "I'll be back in a bit," I tossed over my shoulder, then shifted into high gear, my boots digging into the sand as I pushed myself as hard as my exhausted legs would allow.

Through my bond with Meg, I could sense her concern for me.

I pushed myself even harder until the burn in my muscles was rivaled by the fire in my lungs. Until all thoughts and emotions fled from my mind, and anything leaking through my bond with Meg was buried under a mountain of physical discomfort. Until the only thing that mattered was putting one foot in front of the other. Over, and over, and over again.

[2]

By the time I headed back to the Omega site, I was a sweaty, sandy mess. I'd made seven trips to the pyramid and back, my pace having waned from a sprint to a stumbling jog by the final circuit. I should have stopped sooner, after round four or five, but the thought of seeing Meg and Raiden grappling expertly in the sand had spurred me onward. It would have been just another reminder that I wasn't as strong or capable as I should have been.

Now that my body was fully enmeshed in the throes of exhaustion and all of my wild and flailing emotional energy was spent, I could review my actions—and reactions—with a rational mind. Like a scared child, I had run away. My reaction to Raiden had been one of cowardice, and if I was being honest with myself, it wasn't entirely born of feeling physically deficient.

I was afraid. Of us. Of finding out if there still was an *us*. Of finding out there *wasn't*. I'd always been a coward when it came to matters of the heart, more so as Peri than as Cora, and I felt ashamed of my childish reaction.

So much had changed since we arrived here four days ago. I was a different person. The memories and experiences from all my lifetimes had merged, turning me into someone new. When I was around Raiden, the memories and experiences we shared came to the forefront of my mind, and I felt more like Cora—hesitant, uncertain, weak, and dependent. But when I was around Hades, the opposite happened, and suddenly the Peri traits were dominant, making me feel strong, powerful, and confident as I had been all those millennia ago. I had thought merging my two selves would make my life easier, but now I felt more confused than ever about who I was. And if I didn't even know who I was, how could Raiden or Hades truly know me? How could either of them still love me?

Thankfully, the sparring field behind the Sphinx was vacant by the time I crested the final sand dune and started down the slope toward the front of the monument. I slipped into the Omega site through the entrance nestled between the Sphinx's front legs and was relieved to find the control room relatively empty. Not that it was much of a surprise—it was late, and the others were likely asleep in the closet-sized rooms that counted as living quarters in this particular Olympian site.

Fiona sat on a stool in front of the control panel taking up the entire wall on the right side of the triangular room, her laptop propped on her lap and a jury-rigged cord connecting it to the massive Olympian computer that ran this clandestine site. Her neon orange hair was knotted into a bun on the top of her head, either held in place by a computer stylus or used as a pin cushion for one. With her, it was impossible to say.

Fiona tore her stare from the computer screen as I crossed the space. "Wow," she said, her eyebrows climbing up her forehead. "If I looked up 'hot mess' in the dictionary, I think I'd find a picture of you."

I snorted a laugh, too worn out to be offended. "Thanks."

Fiona winked and made a clicking sound inside her cheek. "Anytime," she murmured, her attention returning to her computer screen. Hades had turned off the electronics dampener, allowing Fiona better access to Olympian tech. She'd been spending as much time as possible jacked into the alien computer system, working on a translation algorithm that would allow her to build an Olympian-to-English interface, giving her access to the full spectrum of Olympian tech. This situation was basically her deepest fantasy come to life, so I was hardly surprised to find her in here burning the midnight oil.

Leaving Fiona to her work, I headed for the door at the far end of the space. The control room was shaped like a cone that had been chopped in half and turned on its side, broadening from the narrow entry point beneath the Sphinx's forelegs to a large, arched metal wall at the far end. Control panels and workstations took up all available space on either side of the room, but the arched metal wall was completely bare, save for the rectangular outline of the door.

The metal door slid open as I neared, revealing the hallway that provided access to all other areas of the Omega site. The layout of this site was very cramped and warren-like, and generally space-ship-y—and with good reason. This site was actually part of the *Tartarus*, the ship that had brought my people here from our dying planet some fourteen millennia ago. Unbeknownst to any but the ruling family—which included the Emperor's scion here on this world, Poseidon; his sister and the traitorous leader of the Order of Amazons, Demeter; and their brother and the bearer of the other half of my heart, Hades—the Omega site had been ejected from the *Tartarus* shortly after arriving here on this planet eons ago and buried underground in a secret location.

It had been planted here as a last resort, a sort of storage locker for our people, should the worst happen. Well, the worst *had* happened, and the consciousnesses of thousands of Olympians were now stored here in the Vault of Souls. For all we knew, this site held the last remnants of my people anywhere in the universe.

The main hallway branched off into many other hallways

leading to different sections of the Omega site. I headed straight for the doorway that led to the personal quarters, waited for it to slide open, and hurried on quiet feet to the third door on the right. I ducked into the room and engaged the *do not disturb* setting as soon as the door panel snicked shut. It wouldn't lock the door, but the red light surrounding the door would let the others know I didn't want visitors.

Blowing out a breath, I leaned back against the door, resting my head against the cool metal, and closed my eyes. Tension I hadn't realized I'd been carrying oozed out of me, and my whole body relaxed. It wasn't that I was avoiding the others exactly; I just didn't know how to be around them anymore. I didn't know how to *be*, period.

With a sigh, I opened my eyes and pushed off from the door. The room was roughly a seven-foot square, with one corner closed off as a washroom of sorts if you could even call a three-foot triangle a washroom. Half of the space was taken up by a long, narrow bed. The other half was open, allowing for use of the various storage drawers and cabinets filling the wall opposite the bed. To call the room cramped was a gross understatement. It was no larger than the average prison cell.

The part of me that had come from Cora struggled with the claustrophobic space, at times, but the part of me that had come from Peri felt at home here. During my first cycle as Peri, spent aboard the *Tartarus* from birth to death, I'd lived the majority of my years in a room just like this.

I peeled off my filthy hoplon suit and sweat-soaked bra and underwear, tossing everything into the sanitizing compartment set in the wall, then tucked into the cramped washroom and ran a shower cycle. When I was finished and squeaky clean, I slid the narrow door of the washroom open only to discover I had a visitor. Immediately, I crossed my arms over my bare chest.

My mom sat on the edge of the bed, her chestnut waves loose around her shoulders and a hand over her eyes. She held what passed for a towel in these parts in her outstretched hand, and a stack of Olympian underclothes and PJs sat on her lap. The manufacturing compartment, really just a small room with what was essentially a huge, highly advanced 3D printer, could produce pretty much anything so long as the machine had adequate fabrication material in its material cartridges beneath the floor. We would need to refill the cartridges eventually, but for now, we had plenty to supply us with pretty much anything we needed.

"Mom!" I stood in the doorway, my heart galloping, and reached out to snag the offered towel. Apparently *do not disturb* didn't apply to nosy mothers. Slightly peeved, I quickly dried off with the small square of moisture wicking fabric, then accepted each piece of clothing as my mom held it out for me to take.

Once I was dressed, I crossed my arms and leaned my shoulder against the wall, eyeing her. "Thanks," I said dryly.

My mom finally looked at me. Concern shadowed her eyes. "How was your run?"

I sighed, letting my arms drop, and rested the side of my head against the wall. "Did you talk to Meg?" The tattletale.

My mom held up a hand, her eyebrows raising. "Now, I know what you're thinking, and no, she didn't tell me anything other than that you went for a run."

"I'm sure," I said, reaching for the brush sitting on the teeny tiny shelf beside the bed. I turned to face the mirror set into the wall and pulled the brush through my long, tangled wet hair with forceful jerks. I could see my mom in the reflection. Our coloring was similar enough—dark, wavy hair, blue eyes, pale skin—that I hadn't questioned our relationship growing up. But now that I knew she wasn't my true biological mother, that though she had carried me in her womb, we didn't actually share any DNA, the differences in our appearances seemed glaringly obvious. The shape of our eyes, our bone structure, even our teeth—there was no similarity to our features whatsoever.

My mom patted the space beside her on the edge of the mattress. "Come here, sweetheart. Sit." She glanced down at the shiny metal floor at her feet. "I'll French braid your hair…"

My arm froze mid-brushstroke, my breath held in my lungs. Never. Never had anyone offered to braid my hair. Not during my life as Cora, when touch had meant extreme pain followed by unconsciousness, or during any lifetime before.

The tiniest smile tugged at the corners of my mom's mouth. "Come on," she urged and, her smile growing and filling with encouragement, she held her hand out for the brush.

I turned around and took a single, hesitant step toward her and handed her the brush. She knew better than anyone how much this would mean to me. Hell, it probably meant just as much to her, a mother who had been unable to offer her daughter a comforting touch for the vast majority of her daughter's life. But the regulator dangling from a chain around my neck fixed all of that, and human touch no longer sent me into psychic overload. I took another step closer, then turned my back to her and eased down onto the floor, settling between her knees.

The first stroke of the brush through my wet hair was far gentler than mine had been. My chin trembled and tears welled on the brim of my eyelids. I closed my eyes, and a tear broke free, streaking down my cheek. How could something so simple make me feel so much?

My mom cleared her throat. "You know, I haven't done this since you were a little girl," she said, her voice thick with emotion. "Your hair was so fine then. It would slip out of the braid by morning and you would end up with the craziest bedhead." She laughed softly.

I couldn't hold back the smile curving my lips. I didn't remember any of that, but it was nice to hear, nonetheless.

The brush snagged on a snarl, jerking my head back, and my eyes snapped open, my neck tensing.

"Sorry," my mom murmured.

I winced as she worked through the snarl. "It's OK."

Silence stretched out between us as she finished brushing my hair, then sectioned it out to begin braiding. Her nails skimming along my scalp sent goosebumps cascading down my neck and back. "How did you wear your hair . . . before?" she asked.

I stared ahead, my eyes locked on the door panel to the washroom as my mom started to braid. I chewed on the inside of my cheek, unsure how to answer.

On the surface, the question seemed benign enough, but I couldn't help but spot the hidden layers of significance. I had been reluctant to talk about my past lifetimes with my mom or any of the others who knew me only as Cora. It seemed to make them uncomfortable, learning things about me that happened so long before they existed. Like I was rubbing their faces in the fact that they didn't really know me, at least, not all of me. With each passing day, I felt the chasm between me and my loved ones expanding. Soon, I feared it would be impossible to cross.

It was so different now than it had been before, when the memories of those previous lifetimes had felt so foreign. But now, those lifetimes were mine—those memories were a part of me, making me who I was today as much as my twenty-six years as Cora Blackthorn had. I could feel myself pulling away from the people I loved before they could push me away.

I took a deep breath, wanting to bridge that chasm. "I usually wore my hair twisted up into a tight bun atop my head," I told my mom, "in accordance with the Amazon dress code."

"Like a ballerina?"

The corner of my mouth tensed, and I exhaled a silent laugh. "Yeah, like a ballerina," I admitted. "It was either that or cut it all off. Long hair is too dangerous in a fight. Too easy for an opponent to grab." My latest match with Meg was proof enough of that. "Plus," I added, "it just gets in the way."

"Ain't that the truth," my mom said. "That's why I never let mine get longer than my shoulders. The Order required women to wear their hair in a bun or braid in the field."

As I thought about her admission, I furrowed my brow. It hadn't occurred to me that maybe my mom could relate to what I was going through. Sure, she didn't have to reconcile eighteen different lifetimes, but she did have to juggle two different identities and deal with the fallout from me, her daughter, discovering she was, in essence, two entirely different people.

I swallowed, then cleared my throat. "Do you miss it?"

My mom's hands stilled, the braid half-finished. "Being in the Order?"

I shook my head gently so as not to hinder her work. "The simplicity of being Diana Blackthorn," I clarified.

My mom chuckled, an unexpected note of bitterness to the laugh. "Being Diana Blackthorn was never simple," she said and resumed braiding. "I was always afraid of slipping up, of saying the wrong thing. Of you finding out the truth . . . and figuring out just how long I'd been lying to you. Don't get me wrong, sweetheart, I have loved every second of being your mom, but I have hated every moment of hiding who I really was." She took a deep breath, sighing on her exhale. "But now the cat's out of the bag, and I'm free to be myself around you. I feel lighter than I have in years."

Out of the corner of my eye, I watched her reach for the hairband on the shelf by the bed. I felt light tugging on the braid as she twisted the band around the ends of my hair. When she was done, she released the braid and rested her hands on my shoulders.

"I—" I took a deep breath and bowed my head, staring down at my hands as I picked at a hangnail. "I don't know if I can do that—be *me*. I'm afraid that if I stop trying to be just Cora, you guys will realize you don't know me anymore." I paused, hesitating before adding, "That you don't love me anymore."

My mom's grip on my shoulders tightened. "Oh, sweetheart .

. .” She turned me around enough that she could see my face. "You're still you," she said, her love for me shining in her deep blue eyes. "You're just *more*." She smiled softly, the skin around her eyes crinkling. "Nobody can ever really know another person. We're all walking through the world, hiding little bits and pieces of ourselves. But one of the most exciting things we get to do during our lifetimes is find those people we love and learn as much as we can about them during the time we have together."

She tucked a flyaway strand of hair behind my ear. "Knowing another person is a process that never ends. There's always more to learn." She laughed softly, brushing her thumbs under my eyes to wipe away my tears. "And, with you, there's just that much more to learn, making knowing you—and loving you—that much more of an adventure."

A stifled laugh-sob escaped from my chest, and I collapsed against my mom, wrapping my arms around her middle. She rubbed my back in slow circles and made soft shushing noises, gently rocking me back and forth. In that moment, this embrace was everything, and I had never loved her more.

After a few minutes of me clinging to my mom, my cries quieted and my shoulders stilled, and I sat back on my heels and wiped the fresh tears from my cheeks. With a sniffle, I stood from the floor and sat beside my mom on the bed. She curled an arm around my waist, and I rested my head on her shoulder.

My mom pressed her cheek against the top of my head. "Now," she started in a tone that made my muscles tense, "do you want to tell me why you've been pushing your body to the point of collapse the past few days?"

I closed my eyes, my gut clenching as I silently thought through my answer. "I have to be better than I am," I started and opened my eyes.

My thoughts zeroed in on the memory of the warning ping coming from the holoscreen a few days ago. The Tsakali were on their way to Earth. My people's ancient enemy—the same brutal, heartless monsters who had not only driven my people from our homeworld, Olympus, but had infected us with a nano-virus that rendered us permanently infertile. They had tried their hardest to obliterate us completely, and now they were coming here, lured by the shiny new chaos stone humans had created, and I feared humanity would suffer the same fate as the Olympians.

"I—" I cleared my throat. "The Tsakali are worse than you could ever imagine," I told my mom. "Not even all the full-powered Amazon warriors on Olympus could defeat their invading force. I know I can't protect this world from them, but maybe if I'm strong enough, I can at least protect you."

"Oh, sweetheart . . ." My mom raised her head, pressing her lips to my hair and tightening her hold on me. "We'll cross that bridge when we come to it."

[3]

The soles of my boots clanged against the metal grating, and the filtered air whooshed in and out of my lungs as I started my twenty-fourth circuit around the ring-shaped Vault of Souls. I'd estimated the hallway running through the Vault of Souls was ten feet across and about half the length of a standard track, so about an eighth of a mile.

The high walls on both sides of the hallway were lined with row after row of small, round recesses, reaching maybe twenty feet overhead. The recesses in the upper half of the walls were empty, the lower half filled with crystalline consciousness orbs swirling with glittering ribbons in every imaginable color. The shade of those ribbons was unique to the Olympian mind contained within each orb, the more muted colors belonging to regular Olympians, the more vibrant, luminous colors belonging to the psychically gifted, like me.

My hoplon suit kept my body more or less sweat-free, but my face and hair were another matter entirely. The stitch in my side convinced me to take a break, and I slowed to a jog, then a walk, and then I stopped, raising one arm over my head to help ease the side ache.

It was late morning, meaning we were trapped down here, beneath the Great Sphinx, for another ten or eleven hours, until full nightfall allowed us to sneak out to the Western Desert for some fresh air. I glanced up at the metal ceiling high overhead. It was so strange to think that a horde of tourists were traipsing around up there right now, exploring the Giza Necropolis, clueless to the alien complex hidden beneath their feet.

Well, maybe not entirely clueless. The fabled Hall of Records was believed by many to exist down here, containing the lost history of ancient Egypt. Some even believed the Hall of Records had been built by Atlanteans. Not quite, but close enough to the truth to have me believing that at some point the ancient Egyptians knew about Hades' hidden underground lair.

With a quick flick of my finger around the stone in my regulator, I deactivated the device, unleashing my psychic gifts. I could sense the crowds of strangers above but tuned them out, focusing on the more familiar minds surrounding me down here. Emi, Hades, Fiona, and my mom were in the control room, while Raiden and Meg were in their respective private quarters, so far as I could tell.

I lowered my arm and cocked my head to the side, sensing something else. It was like a whisper in my ear, tickling the very edges of my psychic senses. The whisper was all around me, and I could have sworn it was coming from the consciousness orbs.

I moved closer to the outer wall, scanning the orbs resting in their individual recesses. One orb stood out in particular, displaying ribbons a hauntingly familiar shade of brilliant coral pink. From handling my own consciousness orb, I knew an Amazon's regulator glowed the same hue as the threads of her stored consciousness. And this color—this consciousness—was achingly familiar to me.

Tentatively, I reached out for the orb and brushed the tips of my fingers over the smooth surface.

The image of a chaotic city street flashed through my mind, overlaying my perception of the space around me.

Startled, I yanked my hand away from the orb. But curiosity got the better of me, and once again, I touched my fingertips to the glassy surface, closing my eyes and focusing on the foreign image.

The city street reappeared, sights and sounds slowly overwhelming my own senses until this place felt just as real as the Vault of Souls, where I had been standing just a moment ago. The city surrounding me reminded me of New York City, at least as I had seen and experienced the famous city in movies and games, but with an alien flare. The skyscrapers were sleeker and more uniform, the people filling the sidewalks a little too tall, their features a little too sharp to be human. This was no city here on Earth; this was an Olympian city, the likes of which I had never visited, and I stared around in wonder.

A woman in a hoplon suit strode past me, the channels running the length of her skin-tight armor glowing a steady coral pink. Other Olympians bowed their heads as the Amazon warrior passed them. The cadence of her stride, matched with the yellow-gold bun atop her head and the telltale swagger, told me exactly who this particular Amazon warrior was—Despoina, my closest friend within the Order of Amazons.

I stumbled forward into a jog to keep up before she could melt into the stream of people. "Des!" I called out, pushing people out of my way as I chased after her. "Despoina!"

Despoina stopped and turned around, her eyes narrowing.

I slowed, then stopped just out of arm's reach of her.

As Despoina looked at me, she shook her head, her eyes slowly widening until wonder transformed her expression. "Peri? How—" Again, she shook her head. "How are you here? You weren't supposed to be integrated into the system with the rest of us."

My brows bunched together, and I tilted my head to the side.

"What system?" I asked, then looked around. "What *is* this place? I was running through the Vault of Souls, and . . ." My attention returned to my old friend.

Despoina smiled, but there was a weariness in her eyes. "This *is* the Vault of Souls. Or, at least, the inside of the vault." She held her arms out to either side of her. "Welcome to Olympus. Hades rigged the system to create a simulated reality pulled from our collective subconsciousness to keep us stimulated during our extended stay here in the ever after." Despoina took a small step closer to me, her brow furrowing as she scanned me from head to toe. "But if you're in the actual Vault of Souls, out in the physical world, does that mean—are you *real*?" Again, she stepped closer, her eyes searching mine. "Did it work? Did Hades resurrect you?"

My mouth opened and then closed again, and I swallowed roughly. If I was understanding Despoina correctly, then she and the rest of the Olympians stored here at the Omega site had been living in a simulated world since the collapse of the Alpha site over twelve thousand years ago. They weren't dormant, as I had been in my lone consciousness orb; they were *existing*, experiencing new things. Their world may have been virtual, but they were very much still alive, and my heart soared with the realization.

Hades and I weren't alone. We *weren't* the last of our people.

"Yeah, I—" I cleared my throat, then nodded my head. "I'm real. I, uh—a lot has happened since . . ." Since I died, I didn't say.

Without warning, Despoina threw her arms around me and pulled me into a tight hug. "I can't believe it's really you!" After a long moment, she released me and took a step back. "Last time Hades communicated with us, he told us everything was going according to plan, but something in his voice told me he wasn't being entirely honest."

I laughed under my breath. "As I said, a lot has happened."

Despoina frowned, but her eyes filled with hope. "Since you're back, does that mean we get to come out soon?"

I inhaled to answer but found I didn't know what to say. Finally, I nodded. "We're working on it," I told her, hoping I was telling the truth.

We were working on a lot of things at the moment, saving Earth from the Tsakali threat *again*, first and foremost among them. But how could I tell her that nothing had changed? That we were right back where we started—or ended—twelve millennia ago, trying to figure out how to evade an imminently invading force?

"I—" I glanced over my shoulder, like I might be able to see the world beyond the simulation. "I should get back, but I just wanted to see you. I never got to thank you for trusting me." We never would have been able to save this planet from destruction by the Tsakali the last time if she hadn't supported me. I flashed her a weak smile. "You've always had my back, Des. Thank you."

"Peri," Despoina said, reaching for me. "Wait—"

I pulled my hand away from the consciousness orb, keeping my eyes closed as the simulated city vanished around me. I hung my head and lowered my hand to my side, my chest rising and falling with each heaving breath. I sensed a presence behind me, both welcome and not. Hades.

My heart beat a little faster, and butterflies fluttered in my belly, my body's instinctive reaction to knowing he was near.

"I was going to tell you about the simulation as soon as you had settled in a little more," Hades said, guessing the reason for my somber mood. Within his mind, I could sense the truth of his words—the purity of his intentions and his regret at the lie of omission.

I opened my eyes and stared at Despoina's consciousness orb, watching the coral-pink ribbons swirl and sway within. She was in there, as alive as me, just lacking a body. What if we could never free her? What if we could never free any of them? What if they were trapped in that simulated reality for all time?

"I didn't realize . . ." Swallowing down my confusing emotions, I raised a hand to activate my regulator. It was hard enough to make sense of my own thoughts without Hades' thoughts invading my head. I took a deep breath, my shoulders relaxing, and turned around to face Hades, tilting my head back to meet his ice-blue eyes.

His elven beauty was as breathtaking as ever, the sharp contours of his face made more pronounced by the way his silver-blond hair was pulled back and tied at the nape of his neck. During my first few lifetimes, I had found Hades incredibly intimidating, but as I had come to know him better, that sense of intimidation had transformed into intrigue, and in time, to desire and love. Once upon a time, I had been ready to give up everything for him, including the relative immortality cloning afforded my people, for the chance to experience something forbidden to the members of the Order of Amazons: love. But before Hades and I could run away together, the Tsakali had brought the illusion of safety surrounding this world crashing down, and our dream of sharing one last lifetime together remained unfulfilled.

Now, we were together again, but the ground beneath our feet was no less shaky. The yearning I had felt for him so long ago still lingered, but I feared we had missed our chance, that what could have been was lost to the ages, just like our people.

"We could bring them back the same way I was brought back," I said, latching onto the safer subject—our people. Talking about *us* was not a conversation I wanted to have right now. My heart was split clean in the middle, and I wasn't ready to deal with the consequences of loving two men. "With surrogates and—and—"

Hades nodded, his expression thoughtful. "We *could* revive them the same way."

I narrowed my eyes. "I'm sensing a *but* in there . . ."

Hades sighed. "But, I don't think we *should* bring them back."

I sucked in a breath to demand an explanation, to argue.

"At least, not right now," Hades added before I could even get started. "I think it would be too risky to implant any Olympian embryos into surrogate human mothers at present with the Tsakali on the way here right now."

Hands on my hips, I pursed my lips, processing his words. "So, what? You think we should wait to see if the Tsakali destroy this planet, *then* think about resurrecting the others?"

Hades shook his head, his mouth forming a thin, flat line. "I think we need to consider evacuating the planet."

"But—but—" I sputtered, my thoughts tumbling over my shock. "But that would require a ship . . . or the gephyra. And we don't have a ship"—the *Tartarus*, which had carried our people here, had been destroyed during the revolution that had claimed my life so long ago—"so you must be talking about the gephyra."

The gephyra was an Olympian device that could create a bridge between distant planets, allowing people to travel far across the universe in the blink of an eye. Only, there was one big problem with that plan—the gephyra required a power source to run, and the chaos fragments that had once powered the gephyra located at the Alpha site were long gone, jettisoned from this planet to lead the Tsakali away the last time they had threatened Earth. Chaos was a unique, sustainable power source the Tsakali coveted above all other things. A new, human-created chaos stone formed from the orichalcum extracted from a meteor that landed on Earth several years ago was the reason we found ourselves in the same bind once again.

My eyes widened, and my lips parted as I stared at Hades, realizing his plan. "You want the chaos stone," I said with absolute certainty.

Hades blinked once, his icy stare steady. "I *need* the chaos stone," he countered. The way he said "need" sent a thrill through my body. "Regardless of what happens when the Tsakali arrive or what we do to prepare for the invasion, without a chaos stone, the Omega site's power core will fail, and then not only will all the Olympian embryos preserved in the Eberus perish, but I will be unable to transfer the consciousness orbs to the Alpha site should evacuation through the gephyra end up being our only option for survival."

I shook my head, grinding my teeth together. "Stop saying 'evacuation' like it's inevitable."

Hades inhaled and exhaled through his nose, his eyes never leaving mine. "It may be the only way to save our people."

"No," I snapped. "It would only save the Olympians, but you're forgetting that they're not my only people on this planet, and there's no way in hell I'm going to abandon humanity to an enemy *we* know everything about while *they* know nothing." Chest heaving, I took a step closer to Hades, drawn in by his intensity. "If that's what you're planning on doing, then know you'll be *evacuating* without me."

Hades clenched his jaw. "Always so idealistic," he hissed. "And so stubborn." His eyes searched mine, his gaze flicking down to my lips, and my stomach did a little flip flop of anticipation.

"Isn't that what you love about me?" My eyes widened as soon as the words left my tongue, and I immediately wished I could suck them back in. My pulse raced, and I flushed.

Hades leaned in closer, his gaze dipping down to my lips once more. "I love many things about you, Peri." His focus returned to my eyes, his own burning with a tightly reined passion. "Would you like me to list them?"

I gulped, then licked my lips. My breaths came faster, my heart hammering in my chest. "I—"

Hades leaned in even closer until our breaths mingled.

Someone cleared a throat nearby.

I jumped back a step, putting some much-needed distance between myself and Hades, and stared at the intruder.

Fiona stood a dozen paces away, her face a mask of discomfort. She flashed me an apologetic smile before shifting her focus to Hades. "Sorry to interrupt, but an alarm is going off," she said, pointing over her shoulder with her thumb. "Just thought you should know."

[4]

Hades and I exchanged a heated look filled with all the unsaid things that hung between us. He had waited thousands of years for my return, and his look made it clear that the passion we'd left unfulfilled all those millennia ago was still there, simmering just under his polished surface. My breath hitched in my lungs as his longing revived mine, fanning embers into flames. I wanted him now, just as much as I had wanted him then.

Without another word, Hades turned on his heel and strode toward the arched doorway, both Fiona and me watching him go. The door panel slid open, and then shut, and only once he was gone could I draw in a full breath.

Fiona whistled and turned back to me. "That man scares me, but in an arousing way," she said, fanning herself with her hand. "If he wasn't already part of your harem, I'd be all over that fine alien ass."

Her crass humor cut through the tension Hades had left in his wake, and my body relaxed. My shoulders slumped, my arms hanging at my sides, and I let my head fall back as I fake cried up at the ceiling. "A, he's not part of my harem. And B, I don't *have* a harem."

Fiona snorted a laugh. "Tell that to the choking sexual tension that clouds the air whenever you're around either of your man toys . . ."

I raised my head to meet Fiona's sparkling green eyes, my stare steady, my expression unamused. "That's really not helpful, Fio."

Taking pity on me, Fiona flashed me an apologetic smile and raised her hands in surrender. "Hey, I just call 'em like I see 'em." She cocked her head to the side, studying me through narrowed eyes. "You know, I think you could do with a little perspective here."

I raised my eyebrows. "Oh, really?"

Fiona pointed to herself and said, "Zero gorgeous guys." She pointed to me. "Two gorgeous guys." She raised one eyebrow. "I mean, how is it fair that the only two beings with penises in this joint are hung up on you? I'm just saying, put yourself in my guy-less shoes. Wouldn't you rather be *you* right now?"

I laughed under my breath and shook my head. Her logic was refreshing, if dangerously skewed by a single variable. "Thanks, Fio. I needed that." I sighed, my attention drifting to the door panel. "I suppose we should go find out what the alarm is about," I said and started toward the door.

Fiona spun on her heel and linked her arm with mine as I passed, falling into step beside me. "Think there's another evil alien race coming to destroy us? Like a two-for-one deal?"

I shrugged. Knowing my luck, I wouldn't put it past the universe to do just that.

"Think they'll be hot?" Fiona mused as the door panel slid open in front of us.

I guffawed, and we stepped into the long hallway that led back to the control room. "The Tsakali? Or the new aliens?"

"Either," Fiona said. "Beggars can't be choosers."

"I honestly couldn't tell you," I admitted. "I've only seen recordings of the Tsakali, and they didn't look much different from you or me." I glanced at Fiona sidelong, a smile tugging at my lips. "What if they're entirely female?"

Fiona groaned. "That would be just my luck—a penis-free invasion of smokin' hot aliens."

I chuckled and once again shook my head, grateful for the distraction provided by Fiona's one-track mind.

Up ahead, the door panel leading to the private quarters slid open, and Emi and Raiden emerged. They spotted us making our way up the passage and paused. Raiden murmured something to his mom, his eyes never leaving me. Emi nodded a hello our way, then turned and headed up the passage to the control room while Raiden stayed behind, apparently waiting for me.

I could feel my cheeks heating the closer Fiona and I drew to Raiden and his appraising gaze.

"Big news, apparently," he said when we reached him, his eyes locking with mine. "Did you hear?"

Fiona and I stopped and exchanged a look.

Anxiety coiled in my gut, suffocating the amusement of only moments ago, and I shook my head.

The corners of Raiden's mouth tensed. "Looks like we have an estimated arrival window for the Tsakali," he shared. "Hades sent my mom to gather everyone."

My eyes widened, and I exchanged another look with Fiona. Panic danced in her emerald stare, and her hold on my arm tightened. As much as she joked about hot aliens, she was as scared of the Tsakali as the rest of us. Maybe more.

"Did he say when?" I asked.

Raiden shook his head and started toward the control room, Fiona and me falling in step beside him. "But my mom had the impression that it wasn't good," Raiden added.

"Awesome," I said, the single word dripping with sarcasm.

The door panel to the control room slid open as we approached.

"Hey, Cora, um . . ." Raiden's fingers curled around my upper arm, and he pulled me to a stop.

Fiona's arm slipped from mine, and she hovered just ahead of me in the hallway.

I looked at Raiden, my eyebrows raised in question. At reading the serious expression on his face, I glanced at Fiona and gave her a quick nod to go on without me. Where Hades had a penchant for rousing my passions, Raiden had always had a calming, grounding effect on me. Hades electrified me, but Raiden soothed me. Neither was better than the other. I enjoyed both. Craved both. *Wanted* both.

But I feared that in the end, I would end up with neither.

"Can we talk?" Raiden asked, drawing my eyes back to him. The question twisted my stomach into knots. "After this, I mean," he clarified, nodding toward the door at the end of the hallway. "In my room?"

I swallowed, practically choking on my reservations. "Yeah, sure," I said and forced a smile. My cheeks heated as I recalled the last time we had been alone together in a bedroom—back in Fiona's castle, half-naked and well on our way to shedding our final few pieces of clothing before being interrupted.

Sensing eyes on me, I glanced up the hallway and found the door panel to the control room open, giving the others a clear view of Raiden and me lingering behind. Hades was watching us.

My blush deepened at the overload of attention, and I averted my gaze to the floor. "Well," I said, clearing my throat and forcing myself to look up at Raiden, "should we find out what all the excitement is about?"

Raiden held an arm out toward the doorway at the end of the passage and the others waiting on us. "After you."

I hurried into the control room, Raiden at my side, and the two of us joined the others gathered near the main control panel on the right side of the room.

Hades' stare lingered on me for longer than was comfortable before he blinked and scanned the rest of the group. "I hoped we would have more time to prepare," he started, "but according to the computer's calculations, the Tsakali will most likely be here in two months." He paused, letting that revelation sink in. "Now that Fiona's translation program is up and running, she has access to the Olympian compendium of knowledge. She's been searching the database for any information regarding the Tsakali on the off chance that she knows of some human technology that could defeat them, but I think it would be best if we all prepared for the worst and readied for evacuation off-world."

"No!" I blurted, shaking my head. "I already told you, we're not abandoning all of humanity to save a species that is, for all intents and purposes, already gone." Betrayal was bitter on my tongue as I thought of Despoina and all the other Olympians stuck in their virtual half-life. But the humans were here, alive *now*, and they deserved a chance to survive this, too.

Hades raised a hand, playing at peacekeeper, but I caught the flash of irritation in his ice-blue eyes. "I mean for evacuation to be a last resort," he clarified.

I crossed my arms over my chest and cocked a hip, not sure I believed him. "Then what would you suggest as our first resort?"

Hades clenched his jaw, his momentary silence locking the two of us in a tense stare down. "I don't know," he admitted. "Yet."

"Well," I said, "I don't think—"

An ear-splitting alarm blared, cutting off my words. All heads turned to the control panel, then rose to the holoscreen higher on the wall, surrounded by a flashing red border.

In my peripheral vision, I saw Hades close his eyes, a pained expression tensing his features.

"What is it?" I asked, my attention snapping back to him. "What now?"

Hades sighed and opened his eyes, reaching out toward the

control panel to tap a button. The alarm silenced, but the holo-screen still flashed red. "The patch on the power core is failing," Hades explained. "I thought it would last longer, but . . ." He sighed again, raising his hands to smooth back his hair unnecessarily. "Running the base at full power isn't helping," he added.

"And you need a chaos stone to fix it," I said, processing the worsening situation out loud.

Hades nodded.

"Alright, then," I said, clapping my hands together. I looked around our small group, meeting each and every pair of eyes. "We can figure out what to do about the Tsakali later. Right now, we have a chaos stone to steal."

[5]

A hush fell over the control room as we considered all that would be involved in a heist to steal the world's single greatest power source. The shiny new chaos stone had been created under the name of *Project Atlantea* by a team of scientists at CERN, the Swiss-based research organization that led the world in advancements in fundamental physics and explored the frontiers of science and technology. According to our latest scan of the planet, the chaos stone was still stored in CERN facilities, no doubt under the highest levels of security.

Stealing the chaos stone wouldn't be easy. Nearly impossible was more like it. But then, *I* was something most people would consider being impossible—an ancient alien psychic warrior, cloned and raised as a human. Meg, another psychic warrior, was just as impossible. And then there was Hades, the Olympian who had been alive for long enough to watch the rise and fall of every major human civilization. If our group of *impossibles* couldn't pull this heist off, no one could.

Hades inhaled deeply, his lips parting as though he was going to say something, but he closed his mouth instead. He glanced at me, but quickly looked away, focusing instead on the flashing red screen.

I narrowed my eyes, studying him. "Hades? What is it?"

Hades dragged his attention back to me and rubbed the back of his neck, hesitating before speaking. "The chaos stone alone will not fix the power core," he finally said. "We need other parts."

That was news to me. So far as I understood, once we had the chaos stone, we could plug it into the Alpha site, bringing the settlement up to full power, and we would be able to fabricate virtually any part we might need to repair the Omega site. Down in the Alpha site's mainframe, we could generate a whole new power core if we wanted. I couldn't imagine needing anything we couldn't just make.

"OK . . ." Arms crossed over my chest, I tapped my index finger against my elbow. "So, we'll search the other Olympian sites for the necessary parts," I said. The Beta site was likely picked over, due to the Zari occupation of the ancient underground settlement, but that still left four more sites here on Earth—the Gamma site, the Delta site, the Epsilon site, and our flagship settlement, the Alpha site.

The corners of Hades' mouth tensed, and I braced myself for bad news. "I've already burned through all the resources on this planet. Since the Omega site was originally part of the *Tartarus*, the tech is far older than that used in any of the other sites here on Atlantis." He shook his head, closing his eyes in a prolonged blink. "I mean, *Earth*." He was quiet for a moment, and the burdens he'd been carrying over the millennia—alone—seemed to weigh down on him. Even with my regulator activated, suppressing my psychic senses, I could practically feel his weariness, and my heart ached for him. "I used what I could to patch the malfunctioning systems," he finally said, "but without the correct parts or materials, I cannot truly fix the power core."

I clenched my jaw. Why couldn't the solution ever be

simple? I took a deep, calming breath, exhaling through my nose. "So, the chaos stone isn't what will fix the power core?" I clarified.

"It won't," Hades said, shaking his head. "But it will make it possible for us to find the parts that will."

I let my head fall back and stared up at the shiny steel ceiling arching overhead. "I was really afraid you were going to say that," I groaned.

"Why?" my mom asked from across the circle. "What's the problem?"

Sighing, I raised my head to look at her. She watched me with curious eyes. "What Hades *isn't* saying is that to find the parts he needs to fix the power core and prevent this whole place from dying, we have to use the gephyra to travel off-world to the lost colonies. That's why we need the chaos stone—it's the only thing on this planet with enough juice to power the gephyra."

"The gephyra," Raiden said, drawing my attention to him, "that's the thing that creates wormholes to other planets?"

"It doesn't create wormholes," Hades started to explain. "It creates bridges. What you call wormholes are actually—"

"The least of our concern," I said, waving a hand to dispel the unnecessary explanation. "Yes, the gephyra allows us to travel to other planets instantly. But what really matters is that we don't know what we'll find on those other planets." After a moment, I added, "Or *who* we'll find."

Meg's brow furrowed as she picked up on the source of my worry through our bond. A moment later, Hades' expression softened as he comprehended my concern, as well, and I shifted my focus to the flashing red screen before I could watch pity fill his eyes.

A team of Amazon warriors had passed through the gephyra over twelve thousand years ago, the day I died, to search the lost colonies for a chaos stone. The Tsakali were headed our way, and we needed the chaos stone to power the *Tartarus'* faster-than-light engines and allow our people to flee this planet. The team had succeeded, and they had been in the process of establishing a bridge back to Earth when the shit hit the fan. Long story short, the team had been stranded on a distant planet.

Because of me. Because I had helped Hades pull out the chaos fragments powering the gephyra, preventing the bridge from forming on our end. Stranding my spearsisters. Damning them.

Those Amazons had likely died on that distant planet, trying to get back here. But as terrifying as that thought was, there was another, scarier option: those Amazons *hadn't* died. That they'd found cryochambers to preserve their bodies, just as Hades had done to survive the passing millennia. That they would awaken and learn what I had done to them, and I would be shunned by the last remnants of my sisterhood.

"If we're traveling to some other planet to search for parts," Fiona said, clueless as to the miserable reality I was facing, "maybe we'll find something else to help us battle these Tsakali space invaders."

"To fight the Tsakali is certain death," Hades said. "Especially for such a primitive species."

Fiona grimaced. "Burn . . ."

"But back to the matter at hand," my mom said. She pointed to Hades. "You're going to be a lot more interested in helping us primitive humans defend our planet from the Tsakali if what remains of your people still, well, remains. Which means we need to find the parts to repair this place"—she swept out an arm to indicate the Omega site— "and to do that, we need to steal the chaos stone."

"Or," Emi cut in, giving my mom an exasperated look, "we could approach the UN and explain the situation like rational, civilized people. They're aware of the Custodes Veritatis, after all. They know life exists elsewhere in the universe. I believe they will listen, assess the threat, and grant us access to the chaos stone."

My mom scoffed. "*Or* they'll lock up Cora and Hades the first chance they get and start slicing them up into little pieces to find out exactly what makes them tick."

Emi settled a flat stare on my mom. "That's a little extreme, don't you think?"

"I think it's better to ask for forgiveness than permission," my mom said, turning her attention from Emi to me, and then to Hades. "If we go to the UN, we'll be wasting valuable time *talking* when we could be *doing*."

"I don't know," Fiona said, chewing on her thumbnail. "I think Emi has a point." She lowered her hand. "I mean, we're going to have to approach world leaders at some point about the impending space invaders, right? Wouldn't it be better to come to them without having to beg for forgiveness?"

I had to agree with Fiona on that point, though I didn't say as much out loud.

My mom searched each of our faces, looking for support. When she found none, she rolled her eyes and crossed her arms over her chest like a sullen teenager. "Fine. We'll do it Em's way."

I flashed my mom an apologetic smile, then looked to Emi. "Right, so, how exactly are we going to get the UN's attention?"

Crickets filled the room.

Suddenly, my mom rubbed her hands together, a manic grin spreading across her face. "I have the perfect plan."

[6]

Henry. Henry Magnusson, leader of the Custodes Veritatis and certifiable asshole, was the key to my mom's perfect plan. He already had the UN's ear, and my mom claimed that feeding him just the right bits of intel about the danger the Tsakali posed to Earth was sure to persuade him to arrange an audience for us with the UN Security Council. If we convinced them that granting us access to the chaos stone would secure the planet's safety, then they would order CERN to hand said chaos stone over.

Or so my mom claimed. I wasn't so sure her crazy plan would work, but Emi agreed with her. Since Emi was by far the more cautious and level-headed of their odd-couple duo—and since nobody else had a better plan—we all agreed, and that was that.

"Alright, so," my mom said, clapping her hands together and rubbing them vigorously back and forth, "I'll go make some calls, get things rolling." She turned toward the stairway that would carry her up to the exit located between the Sphinx's forelegs. "We'll need transport, and—"

I snagged her arm before she could pass me. "Mom, wait."

She looked at me, her eyebrows raised in question.

"It's the middle of the day." I sent a pointed look up toward the ceiling and the great limestone monument acting as a tourist magnet directly above us before releasing her arm. "There's a crap-ton of people up there . . ."

My mom's lips parted, her eyes widening. "Oh, right." She laughed to herself and shook her head. "It's easy to lose track of time down here." She turned around and made a beeline for Emi, stopping to place a hand on Emi's arm. "Help me figure out the best thing to say to Henry?"

Emi smiled faintly and nodded, and the two headed for the door panel leading deeper into the Omega site. Now that things were winding down, it was impossible for me not to notice Raiden's attention had landed on me, and my mind raced to come up with some reason to postpone our little chat. Why did the Custodes Veritatis never attack when it was convenient for me—like when I was trying to avoid difficult personal conversations?

"Oh, and Diana," Hades called after my mom.

My heart beat faster as I hoped that whatever Hades was about to say would delay the inevitable just a little bit longer.

My mom and Emi paused just this side of the doorway to look back at Hades.

"Transport will not be necessary," Hades informed her. "We can take the *Argo*."

My mom exchanged a look with Emi, curiosity written all over their faces. "And what, pray tell, is the *Argo*?"

"It's a paralus," I said, stepping in with an explanation that would make sense to modern people. "It's an all-terrain Olympian craft built for land, sea, and air travel, and it's equipped with cloaking technology, so we'll be able to travel undetected."

My mom raised one eyebrow, her curiosity amplified to intrigue. "Well now, isn't that handy." Her stare fixed on Hades.

"Now that I think of it, I think it would be wise to make a list of the Olympian technologies you would be willing to trade for access to the chaos stone. Nearly every leader in this world would give their left arm to get their hands on something like the *Argo*."

"As you say," Hades said with a bow of his head. "I shall consider such a list carefully."

Raiden's stare was a laser burning a hole in the side of my face.

A brilliant idea popped into my head, and I blurted, "I need a shower." Eyes locked on the door panel, I hurried from the control room. Once I had ducked into the safety of my private quarters, I stood in the middle of the cramped space and stared at the wall, my heart hammering in my chest.

I was a coward. I had always been a coward when it came to matters of the heart. One needed only to ask Hades why literal lifetimes of a deepening emotional connection and burning desire had gone unfulfilled.

I jumped at a knock on the door, spinning around and hugging my middle. It was Raiden, it had to be. He was here to call me out on my cowardice. To force me to confront the thing I had been running from since my two selves had become one— my heart.

My knees wobbled as I made my way back to the door. I took a single, shaky deep breath, relaxed my arms, then pressed the button on the side of the door. The panel slid open with a faint *whoosh*.

Raiden stood in the hallway, a hesitant smile curving his full lips, though it did nothing to ease the tension in his warm, brown eyes.

"Oh, hey," I said, aiming for nonchalance and hitting awkward perfectly.

Raiden's stare slid past me to the glorified closet of a room behind me. "Hey, Cora. Can I—" He pointed to the doorway.

"Oh!" I said, feigning surprise. Heat crawled up my neck and suffused my cheeks. "Yeah, of course. Sorry, I forgot about our, um—that we were going to talk." Brow furrowing, I shook my head and stepped out of the way. I made a weak gesture with my arm, inviting him into the cramped space.

Raiden scanned the room as he entered, his eyes lingering on the unmade bed. The door panel snicked shut behind him. His scrutiny made me all too aware that this was his first time in here since we arrived five days ago. "So, this place was originally part of the *Tartarus*," he said, his watchful gaze finally landing on me. "I guess that explains why it feels like we're trapped in a spaceship,"

Nodding, I took a step backward to put some space between us. With his big body in here, the room seemed to shrink by the second. My shoulder blades touched the wall of storage compartments opposite the bed, and I leaned into it, tucking my hands behind my back. My stare drifted down to Raiden's scuffed combat boots, looking so at odds with the shiny metal floor.

"Being here has been giving me flashbacks to my first cycle." I glanced up at his face, just for a second. "I mean, my first lifetime. I spent all sixty years living on the *Tartarus*. It's hard to shake the feeling that we're actually hurtling through space right now, not parked on Earth, and that the world out there is all just a dream."

Raiden leaned his shoulder against the door and crossed his arms over his chest, making his biceps bulge. I didn't need to be looking at his face to know his stare was fixed on me. "Is that what this life feels like to you?" he asked. "Like a dream?"

The notes of loss and fear in his tone drew my eyes up to his. Cracks formed in my heart, and I opened my mouth, then shut it and shook my head. "That's not what I meant. It's just—" Again, I shook my head. Shoulders slumping, I pushed off the wall and trudged over to the bed. I sat on the edge, leaning forward to rest my forearms on my thighs, and sighed. "It's hard to explain," I said, rubbing my hands over my face. Hiding from him.

Raiden sat beside me on the bed, close, but not touching. An electrified charge seemed to connect us, nonetheless.

I stiffened, my hands glued to my face.

"Listen, Cora," Raiden started, his voice a gentle rumble. "I get that you might need some space after everything that happened, and I know Peri isn't exactly my biggest fan. The situation has changed, and I just want you to know I don't expect anything from you." He was quiet for a moment. "At least, nothing like, well, you know . . ."

My blush resurfaced, and I groaned, hunching in on myself further. I peered at him from between my fingers. "You talk about Peri like she's someone else," I said, my words slow and cautious. I lowered my hands, settling them on my knees, and looked at Raiden head-on. "Raiden, she's *me*."

Raiden's jaw clenched, and he swallowed repeatedly, his gaze leaving mine to search the ceiling. "So, my Cora really is gone," he said, his voice monotone.

I squeezed my eyes shut, willing the sting of tears to abate. I considered telling him yes. Telling him his Cora was gone. Maybe that would be easier. He could mourn the girl he'd grown up with and move on. He could mourn me. Except, I was still here. Still me. And I didn't want him to move on. Even thinking about losing him made me feel ill.

Opening my eyes, I looked at Raiden, studying the strong lines of his profile until I worked up the nerve to admit the truth. "Raiden, I *am* your Cora."

He was quiet for a long moment. We both were. But finally, he looked at me and said the thing that must have been picking away at him. "But you're also *his* Peri."

I searched his eyes for several heartbeats, then sighed and rubbed the back of my neck with one hand. "Yeah, I am," I said, a slight bite to my words. "I'm his Peri, and I'm your Cora. But it's not like I'm two people, like how you're thinking of it. It's more like I'm one person who's lived for a really, really long time, and who got knocked on the head twenty-six years ago and forgot who she was but kept on living. But now that my head is cleared and the amnesia is gone, those years are integrated into the rest of my life, and I'm back to just being me." I let out a breathy laugh and shook my head. "I don't know if that made any sense at all."

Raiden nodded to himself. "It does, kind of," he said. "It's just hard for me to wrap my head around the fact that you've lived so many lifetimes. I mean, you look good for a nine-hundred-year-old."

I snorted a laugh. I didn't have the heart to tell him a little over one thousand would have been more accurate. "I *do* look good, don't I?"

Raiden flashed me a lopsided smile. "I just—I know you've been avoiding me. And I get it. This situation is awkward. I mean, I always thought if I found myself in this kind of situation, I'd just bow out. Like, nothing is worth that kind of drama."

My stare dropped to the floor, and the air lodged in my lungs. This was it. He was going to end things between us, and I could hardly blame him for doing it.

Raiden blew out a breath and scrubbed his hands over his face. When he finally lowered his hands, he slumped forward. "I don't know how to compete with someone who quite literally brought you back from the dead," he said. "I mean, the guy spent thousands of years trying to bring you back. I just—" He shook his head. "I can't compete with that."

I peeked at Raiden out of the corner of my eye. "Why does it have to be a competition?"

A dry laugh shook Raiden's chest. "Polygamy just isn't my thing."

"Polyandry," I corrected. "Polygamy is one man with multiple women. Polyandry is, well, the opposite."

Raiden glanced at me, but his stare slid back to the wall of storage compartments in front of us. "I can wait," he said. "For you to decide, I mean. For this new, integrated you to figure out what you want."

I stared up at the ceiling, my eyes stinging with tears.

This. This right here was why I'd been doing everything I could to avoid this conversation. Because so long as we didn't actually talk about *us*, whatever we had shared—or almost shared—wouldn't be over.

"What if I love you both the same?" I asked, my voice thick with emotion. I wiped under my eyes before the tears could fall. "What if I can't decide?"

Raiden laughed, the sound hollow and devoid of humor, and shook his head. "You can't have both of us, Cora. It doesn't work that way."

"But it could," I ventured, my voice small.

"*I* don't work that way," Raiden countered.

I opened my mouth but struggled with how to respond. "Well, I do," I finally told him. There it was. The truth laid at his feet. "There's no such thing as monogamy in Olympian culture."

Raiden's head snapped around and he looked at me, clearly taken aback. "Seriously?" His eyebrows climbed up his forehead. "That must've been fun." The corner of his mouth lifted. "And here I'd thought I was the experienced one in this relationship, but nine hundred years of non-monogamy, well . . ."

I stared down at my hands, picking at my nails. "Amazons weren't allowed romantic relationships," I told him. "Demeter didn't want anything distracting us . . . getting in the way of our mission. So, don't worry—you still win in the experience department."

Raiden sat up straighter. "Wait, are you saying you've never —" He cleared his throat. "That you and Hades never . . ."

My neck and cheeks were suddenly on fire. "I'm saying I've never dot-dot-dotted with anyone," I admitted.

Raiden blinked, shook his head, and blinked again. "Wow."

"Yep," I said, exhaling heavily. "But I do think you're right that I need to take some time to just be me . . . on my own." I was quiet for a moment. "I don't really know how to be around either you or Hades right now, so I just end up running away from both of you." I flashed Raiden a weak smile. "I'm sorry I've been avoiding you. Clearly, I'm about as emotionally developed as a twelve-year-old."

Raiden chuckled, and the sound sent relief rushing through me. We hadn't actually figured anything out, but at least the air was cleared. Or moderately less cloudy. He slung his arm over my shoulders and pulled me against his side, and I rested my head on his shoulder. It felt good to be so close to him. It felt right.

"I missed you," I said softly.

Raiden pressed a kiss to the top of my head. "Missed you, too."

I stood at the top of the loading ramp in the aft of the *Argo* and worried my bottom lip as I watched Raiden, Emi, and my mom exit the ship to the sunlit lawn, slinking into a patch of leafy trees nearby. The *Argo* was roughly the size of a school bus, only far more aerodynamic, with sleek, stubby wings that jutted out from the sides, and it didn't look like anything that had ever been made by man. It practically screamed *alien spaceship*; the only thing that would have stood out even more as being not of this world was a flying saucer.

The *Argo* was currently parked in a large copse of trees on the lawn of the Parc de l'Ariana, the manicured park in front of the United Nations Office in Geneva. The ship was cloaked to virtual invisibility, hiding it from the morning foot traffic, which meant we could hunker down within the safety of the ship while we waited for the others to meet with the UN Security Council.

All it had taken was an anonymous email to Henry with a set of coordinates pointing to the location of the incoming Tsakali forces and a phone number. Within fifteen minutes of sending the message, my mom was talking to him on the phone. Another fifteen minutes, and he was off to arrange a meeting for us with the UN Security Council for the following morning. And now we were here.

My mom had been right, and I supposed I shouldn't have been surprised by the outcome. As the Primicerius of the Custodes Veritatis, Henry had a better idea than most humans of what was really out there. Of what might be coming. Of not only the physical threat to mankind but the threat to something far more fragile—civilization. The primary purpose of the Custodes Veritatis, warped as it had become over the years from its original purpose, was to protect humanity from the truth—that humans are not alone in the universe. That they are not special, or chosen, or blessed. That they are merely life-forms, evolved to reach a higher level of thinking. If the truth were ever to get out, humans might not need the Tsakali to destroy them. They might just do it themselves.

The loading ramp started to rise, and I backed up, watching the trio's retreating backs until the ramp cut off my view. I was desperate to be with them, to protect them as they headed into the belly of the beast, but Raiden and my mom had convinced me it was too dangerous. Henry would do almost anything to get his hands on me, and it was the less risky gamble to send my loved ones in there without me, assuming UN security could protect them, than to walk in there myself.

I turned to make my way back up to the front of the ship. The interior of the *Argo* displayed the usual Olympian utilitarian design and sleek aesthetics, with bench seating along either side and storage compartments underfoot. Two pilot-style chairs occupied the front cockpit area, surrounded by a complex control panel with buttons, switches, and holoscreens galore—everything one might need to take this ship from sea to land to air. Everything was shiny steel reinforced with golden orichalcum.

I passed Meg, perched on a cushy bench seat along the side of the ship, studying a floor plan on the screen of Fiona's tablet. She glanced up at me as I passed, flashing me a quick smile.

Fiona sat on the floor near her feet, her legs sprawled in front of her and her laptop on her thighs, her fingers clicking away on the keys. Both were researching the nearby CERN facility where the chaos stone had been created and was being stored, Meg focusing on the layout of the *Atlantea Project* facility and Fiona on the facility's security measures.

Diplomacy was plan A. Should things go south in the meeting with the UN Security Council, grand larceny was plan B.

I reclaimed the vacant seat beside Hades and craned my neck to watch my mom, Emi, and Raiden through the windshield. They crossed the vast expanse of lush green grass toward the sprawling, pale stone UN building, carrying pieces of my heart with them. I watched them until they disappeared into the building, and then I settled in to wait.

"If anything happens to them in there . . ." I blew out a breath and leaned my head back against the headrest. "You know, sometimes I think Demeter was onto something, with her anti-love relationship ban. Maybe she was right and love really is a weakness. I never understood it until now, but maybe she was protecting us from the pain of grief."

Hades scoffed. "She wasn't protecting you," he said bitterly. "She was controlling you."

I glanced at him sidelong, surprised by the vitriol in his voice.

"My sister was a narcissist who required absolute devotion," he said, staring out through the windshield. "She couldn't handle sharing her followers. Her fragile ego couldn't handle even one of you straying from her absolute authority. She brainwashed you all into thinking love was a weakness, but she was wrong."

I raised my eyebrows, intrigued by Hades' words.

He turned his face to me, his ice-blue stare entrancing me. "I see you now, surrounded by those you love, and you burn with purpose—far more than anything Demeter could have instilled within you. You would protect these people at any cost. That is not a weakness. That is a strength."

I flushed at the praise and looked down at my hands.

Hades reached across the space separating our seats and gently touched my chin, raising my face so I was once more looking at him. His touch sent a thrill through me, and I closed my eyes, savoring this moment. "Demeter is gone," he said, his voice low. "Don't let her control you still. You are far stronger—and better—than she ever was."

I swallowed roughly and opened my eyes, my stare locking with his. "She made me what I am," I said, my voice weak.

"No," Hades said, laughing under his breath and shaking his head. He pulled his hand back. "No, she didn't. She merely gave you the tools you needed to make yourself into the strongest of the Amazons. *You* did that, not her."

Mulling over Hades' words, I returned to staring out the windshield. Hades fell silent beside me, seeming to sense that I needed some time to process what he had said.

The sun climbed higher in the sky as we sat there, and noon came and went. The only sound within the ship was the hushed voices of Meg and Fiona as the two shared information and discussed heist strategy. The tension within me ramped up with each passing hour that the others remained out of sight within the UN building.

"Cora?" my mom said over the ship's communication system.

Her voice jarred me out of a trance, and I started in my seat. I almost thought I had imagined it until she spoke again.

"Are you there?" she asked.

Hades leaned forward, tapping the button that would turn on two-way communication.

I flashed him a quick smile, relief flooding me. "Yeah, Mom, I'm here," I said, sitting up straighter. I glanced down at the watch she'd lent me on my wrist. It was nearly two o'clock in the afternoon. They had been in there for almost five hours. "How's it going in there?"

My mom was quiet for a long moment. "It's going . . ." She sighed.

I exchanged a wary look with Hades. "That doesn't sound good."

"They're willing to listen," she said, exasperation edging into her tone. "Henry has twisted this whole thing around in an attempt to get what he wants."

I narrowed my eyes. "Which is what, exactly?"

Again, my mom fell silent for long seconds. Finally, she answered. "You, Cora. He wants you."

I pressed my lips together, breathing deeply through my nose. I refused to look at Hades, though I could feel his searching stare searing into the side of my face.

"He's poisoned the Security Council against me," my mom said, "convincing them I'm a duplicitous mercenary, as likely trying to steal the chaos stone for personal gain as delivering an honest warning." With my mom's track record, it was a hard claim to dispute.

"Bastard," I practically growled.

"Did they check the coordinates we sent?" Hades asked, cutting in with a level-headed question while I silently fumed.

"Yes," my mom said. "And they can see that *something* is headed our way, but the satellites they have access to aren't strong enough to determine what it is or to allow them to predict how close it will come to Earth—let alone when. Their closest projections estimate the 'space object' won't arrive for another ten thousand years, at least."

"They're not accounting for the FTL jumps," Hades countered, a sharp edge to his words.

"Obviously," my mom agreed. "And I told them that the Tsakali don't travel at a consistent speed, but . . ." Again, she sighed. "They want proof."

I looked at Hades, my eyes locking with his as fear pooled in my belly. I knew where this was going, but I had to ask, anyway. "Proof of what, exactly?"

"That you exist. That this isn't some big conspiracy theory hoax," my mom said. "They want an Olympian—in here—confirming what I'm telling them. And they want access to Olympian satellites, so they can better assess the situation."

I was already shaking my head before my mom finished speaking. The fear in my gut was clawing up my chest, reaching for my heart. If either Hades or I went in there, there was no guarantee we would make it back out. I couldn't lose Hades, not when I'd only just found him again.

"I'll go," Hades said, the words ringing with finality.

"No," I snapped. "No way."

"It has to be me," Hades said, his eyes traveling over the lines of my face like he was memorizing them. "You look too much like them. They won't believe you aren't of this world."

I gripped the armrests of my chair with claw-like fingers, my fear for him warping into a far more manageable emotion: anger. "And whose fault is that?"

"We designed you, all of you, to blend in, you know that," he said, speaking of the engineered Olympian like me, those created on board the *Tartarus* during the long trip to Earth. "In nine out of ten scenarios, that's an advantage," he added.

"But not in this scenario," I quietly seethed. I knew he was right—about all of it—and I hated it.

"No," Hades agreed, the calm to my storm. "Not in this scenario." His stare was steady, his voice even. "If you go in there, they'll want to run tests. They'll want further proof that you're different."

A cruel smile twisted my lips, and I tapped the stone of my activated regulator with the nail of my index finger. "That should be easy enough."

Hades raised an eyebrow, and his smug expression suggested

I had just made his point for him. "Yes, you'll show them just how different you are, and in doing so, you'll frighten them so much that they'll lock you away. You will be the only danger they can see, the one in the same room as them, not the one galaxies away. They will not understand you, so they will destroy you."

I slumped in my seat as his words hit home.

"You forget that I have spent millennia studying these creatures," he reminded me, his expression grim, "and their greatest weakness is fearing that which they do not understand."

I clenched my jaw but held my tongue, crossing my arms over my chest. "Fine, you go," I said. "Dazzle them with your otherness."

Hades bowed his head, grateful I had come around.

I sat up straighter, my stare hardening to a challenge as an idea formed in my mind. "But I'm coming with you," I said and grinned. "They can't hurt what they can't see."

[8]

Hades and I stood side by side at the back of the *Argo*, waiting as the loading ramp lowered to the ground. Hades controlled the ramp from the holoband wrapped around his forearm, connecting him to the ship's controls. Fiona and Meg watched us from further in the ship, their faces twin masks of worry. Meg's concern leaked in through our bond, and I had to concentrate to shove the invading emotion aside.

Hades had given Fiona a crash course in manning the ship, so they would be able to flee should the worst happen, and we were captured or killed. Their worry wasn't for themselves. It was all for us.

Beside me, Hades fidgeted with the cuff of his sleeve. His shimmering, fine-woven white tunic and trousers looked as alien as the rest of him—almost like he belonged, but not quite. "I still think it's unnecessary for you to come—"

I silenced him with a look.

Hades was a fool if he thought I would let him walk into a hornet's nest all on his own. It wasn't that he was incapable of taking care of himself. He was a prince of Olympus, raised during a time of war. His body had been trained as well as his mind. If push came to shove, he could handle himself in a fight as well as Raiden or pretty much any other human soldier out there. Better, probably, considering the amount of time he had had to train his body and hone his skills. But Hades had a romantic idea of humanity. Humans were like children in his mind—mischievous, perhaps, but relatively harmless. I wasn't going with him purely out of fear of an external threat; I was going with him to save him from himself.

"You will remain concealed," he said, the command bred into him through his royal blood lacing his words.

I eyed him sidelong. "That's the deal."

To prove just how compliant I could be, I raised one hand, tracing the outline of the stone in my regulator to deactivate the device and unleash my psychic gifts. With a focused thought, I activated my hoplon suit's stealth mode, sending a surge of psychic energy into the suit to bend the light around me, making me as invisible as the ship in which we stood. It took a steady stream of psychic energy to maintain the illusion—energy I didn't necessarily have to spare, considering the heist that might be happening in a little bit—but I wasn't willing to risk sending Hades in there alone. He was too important, not only to me but to our people and to this world, even if humanity didn't know it or was too stubborn to see it.

"Happy?" I asked pointedly.

Hades studied the place where I had been—still was, just not to his or anyone else's eyes.

"That is *so* cool," Fiona said, her voice hushed.

"You take the lead," I told Hades. "I'm right behind you."

Huffing out a breath, his final show of dissatisfaction, Hades started down the loading ramp. I followed.

A half-dozen armed guards awaited Hades on the landing in front of the palatial UN building, and as we ascended the broad, carved stone steps, they fanned out to receive and surround him. I hung back, remaining outside their circle, so as not to accidentally bump into any of them and give away my presence.

The guards escorted Hades into the building through a glass door, three preceding him and three following. I snuck in before the final guard could shut the door.

The entry hall was typical of a fancy government-type building, with high coffered ceilings and an excess of stonework. Pale, polished marble tiled the floor, bordered by white-veined-black marble around the edges. The walls were trimmed with red marble and more of the same black stone. Floor-to-ceiling windows displayed a view of the Parc de l'Ariana, and I would have been able to see the *Argo* parked amongst the trees down the gently sloping lawn, had the ship not been cloaked. It was a comfort to know the ship truly was invisible to the naked eye.

The guards led Hades into a hallway that branched around to the side of the building, then through a pair of tall wooden doors from a quartet set in the wall on our left. This time, I slipped in ahead of the guards and Hades, stepping off to the side to move out of their path.

The chamber beyond was cavernous, the centerpiece being the huge white oak horseshoe-shaped table filling the middle of the floor. Dozens of important looking people sat both at the table and in the two rows of chairs set up behind those at the table. Red, theater-style seating sloped upward from the open end of the horseshoe table, though all those seats were empty save for the two in the front, occupied by Emi and Raiden. My mom and Henry sat at a small table that had been set up near the opening of the larger table. From the looks of it, my mom had scooted her chair as far from Henry's as possible. Two more guards stood sentry at the quartet of doors set in the opposite wall. The air was thick with an unsettling cocktail of emotions: anxiety and fear, excitement and skepticism, and the underlying thread of greed.

All eyes locked on Hades as he entered the chamber, and the

greed wafting off the Security Council and their assistants ratcheted up a notch. The spike of excited interest as hungry stares latched onto Hades set my teeth on edge. He was an object to them. A curiosity. A *thing*.

Tension coiled in my muscles, and I clenched my jaw, my nostril flaring.

Hades stopped three steps into the room, and his escort of guards fanned out to either side of him. He stood tall and proud, playing the part of the alien prince to perfection. The skepticism I had sensed only moments ago faded in the face of his otherness.

A delegate seated near the middle of the horseshoe table stood, a petite middle-aged woman with dark hair and shadowed eyes, followed by the rest of the delegates in a wave. The assistants and advisors seated behind them followed suit. Henry stood as well, his eyes gleaming and greedy as he stared at Hades, though my mom remained seated.

"Welcome, Mr. Hades," the petite brunette delegate intoned, her English accented by her native tongue, which I was fairly certain was Russian. A quick peek into her mind confirmed my guess.

One of the assistants seated in the second row carried a chair to the opening of the horseshoe table and set it directly in front of my mom's smaller table.

The Russian delegate gestured to the chair with a sweep of her arm. "Please, come forward and take a seat." She smiled, though her eyes remained guarded. "As I'm sure you can imagine, we have many questions for you."

Hades crossed the room, heading for the designated chair, but stopped beside the smaller table and stared down his nose at Henry. "Henry Magnusson, I presume?" Hades said, his voice razor sharp. He knew well enough what had become of the Custodes Veritatis, an organization he had set up nearly three thousand years ago to help guide humanity toward a brighter future—one that would allow for a reemergence of the Olympian species. How far the ancient organization had fallen, their purpose grossly warped by time and human greed.

It was impossible to pick out Henry's emotions from the rest of the crowd without dipping into his mind, and I couldn't risk him sensing my presence. He had felt my psychic touch before, and there was a good chance he would recognize it again. Not that I would have needed psychic gifts to read him right now. His awe at being addressed by name not just by an Olympian, but by the creator of the group to which he had devoted his life was written across his face.

Hades shook his head and sniffed a laugh. "I had such high hopes for your organization," he said, his words dripping with disapproval.

The color drained from Henry's face along with his awe.

"You are my greatest disappointment," Hades added before continuing toward the chair, leaving Henry to stare after him, shaken to the core.

I smirked. Served him right, the douche.

Hades sat, turning the simple blue chair into a throne. All around him, the humans regained their seats, as well.

I surveyed the room once more, weighing the emotions of all in attendance and sampling the surface thoughts of a few of the delegates seated at the horseshoe table. So far, so good. Nobody was planning anything that would harm Hades or my mom, Emi, and Raiden. Still, I silently drew my doru from the sheath on my back and extended it to full length, just in case.

"Mr. Hades," the Russian delegate began.

"*Prince* Hades . . . of Olympus," Hades corrected the woman, bowing his head in greeting. "At your service."

The Russian delegate cleared her throat, exchanged uncertain looks with the surrounding delegates, and flashed Hades an uncertain smile. "Prince Hades—"

"But *you* may call me 'Hades'," he interrupted with a charming curve of his lips.

The Russian delegate blushed, and a few of the other delegates tittered. The Russian delegate cleared her throat. "Hades," she began, "my name is Irina Petrov. I am the president of the Security Council, and I will be leading this interview." She licked her lips. "We understand that you are among the last of your kind—you and one called 'Persephone' who was raised as a human by Ms. Blackthorn, seated behind you. Is this correct?"

"On this planet, yes, we are the last of our kind," Hades confirmed. "Though the minds of many more of my people reside in a safe location here on Earth."

"And where is that, exactly?" Irina asked.

Hades took his time in responding. He inhaled, then leaned forward, resting his forearms on his knees. "I believe that Ms. Blackthorn has already explained the situation to you," he started, "and to rehash all that has already been covered would be a great waste of time, both yours and mine." He paused, surveying the faces of the delegates seated around the long, curved table. "The matter of the Tsakali threat is quite urgent. If you are not prepared to discuss strategy, then I must consider this planet a lost cause and be on my way. If you are unwilling to cooperate, I cannot save your people, but I can still save mine."

Outrage overwhelmed all other emotions in the room, and the delegates burst into hushed admonishments and urgent side conversations.

Irina banged her gavel on the stand on the table in front of her three times, and the room quieted. She flashed Hades a tight-lipped smile. "We understand that these 'Tsakali' are your ancient enemy and that they drove you and your people away from your home planet some . . ." She flipped through the notepad on the table in front of her "Thirteen thousand years ago."

Hades nodded once. "That is correct."

Irina released the pages of her notepad, letting them fall back in place. "Then it stands to reason that you have drawn them here, as you are the common element."

I rolled my eyes. She was wasting time and energy with this line of questioning.

"That is incorrect," Hades said, his voice even. "*You* have drawn them here by dabbling in forces you do not understand. You created a chaos stone—what you call the Atlantea Project— alerting the Tsakali to your existence, and now they are coming for you."

Irina bristled. "You must give us access to your technology so we may prepare for the coming invasion."

Hades laughed, deep and booming, the sound echoing throughout the chamber. "Invasion?" he said, shaking his head as he straightened in his chair. "No, this will not be an invasion. It will be an annihilation. You cannot fight them. You will not win. But you are right about one thing—you need my people's technology. Your only hope at survival is to give me the chaos stone so I might search the lost Olympian colonies for the weapon my people created after our world was destroyed. Only that can defeat the Tsakali."

I frowned to myself, appreciating the clever lie. No such weapon existed.

"With your current technology," Hades continued, "you will not stand a chance against them. Without our weapon, once they arrive, you are already dead."

Irina's stare had hardened as Hades spoke. She drew herself up to her full seated height. "Simply because your people could not beat them does not mean we cannot." Her eyes narrowed. "Or perhaps this is all a ruse, and the invading force is led by your own people, and this 'chaos stone' as you call it is the only way for us to defend ourselves from your people. For all we know, *you* are the enemy at the gates. We have no reason to trust you."

I cringed, hating her logic but understanding it, nonetheless.

Hades tilted his head to the side, acknowledging the merit of her argument. "If you do not trust me," Hades told her, "you will die."

Irina stiffened, and the undercurrent of fear wafting through the room increased until it was the dominant emotion. Delegates and assistants shifted in their seats. Tense looks were exchanged, along with a few hushed words.

"Is that a threat?" Irina asked Hades.

He shook his head, laughing bitterly. "Merely a statement of truth. In all honesty, I couldn't care less about the humans of this planet. You have let me down time and time again. If I were to have my way, I would take what remains of my people and leave you to your fate." He fell quiet, letting the conviction in his words sink in. "But it is not only up to me, and Persephone has a soft spot for humanity. We will help you if we can. I have promised her that much. But to do that, we need the chaos stone."

I drew in a deep breath and held it in the sudden silence filling the room. Hades was playing hardball, attempting to stiff-arm the Security Council into giving him what he wanted. His strategy was either brilliant, or absolute rubbish, and I honestly wasn't sure how it would play out.

Irina stared at Hades, visibly flustered by the frank admission of his outright disregard for human life.

Henry pushed back his chair and stood, drawing the delegates' focus from Hades to him. "Offer them collateral," he said.

Hades turned his head to peer over his shoulder at the Primicerius of the Custodes Veritatis.

"Offer them collateral," Henry repeated, "and perhaps they will trust you." He clasped his hands together behind his back. "Give up the location of where you are storing what remains of your people, and this council *may* consider your request for access to the chaos stone."

"Never," Hades hissed, standing abruptly.

Irina raised a hand, signaling for the guards to move in closer. "Please sit down, Hades," she said, more of a command than a request. "We cannot allow you to leave until our negotiations have reached a satisfactory conclusion."

"I am done negotiating," Hades informed her, straightening his gleaming tunic. He started toward the doors through which we had entered the chamber.

"No, you're not," Irina said. "Detain him!"

Two of the guards who had escorted us into the chamber closed in on Hades, taking hold of his arms and wrenching them behind his back. The pain in his shoulders forced Hades to bend forward.

My mom jumped to her feet, her chair toppling over backward. "What are you doing?" she shouted. She started around the table, heading for Hades.

Another guard swooped in on her, yanking her back a few steps with his tight grip on her arm.

Emi and Raiden stood, preparing to do something really stupid.

Irina's lips spread into a predatory grin. "You will find that we mere humans can be quite resourceful when backed into a corner, *Prince* Hades," she said, her voice hard. "It would have been easier if you had cooperated willingly, but we have other ways of getting the information we need."

"Are you crazy?" my mom screeched, fighting against her guard's hold. "He's trying to *help* you."

"Desperate times, Ms. Blackthorn," Irina said, not taking her eyes off Hades.

I rushed forward, sneaking into the space at the center of the horseshoe table, and settled into a defensive stance. I created a telepathic link with Hades, my mom, Emi, and Raiden. *"When I say 'now', drop to the floor,"* I told them in their minds. With a thought, I made myself visible and loosed a muted energy blast at the mural on the wall behind Irina.

For a single heartbeat, everyone in the chamber froze, their attention shifting to me.

"Now!" I shouted before the panic of being under attack could set in and the guards could regroup and retaliate.

Emi and Raiden dropped to the floor unheeded, covering the backs of their heads with their hands. The guards holding onto my mom and Hades were too shocked by my energy blast to stop either of them from dropping.

I slammed the butt of the doru onto the floor, sending out a psychic shock wave at waist height that would temporarily stun every person it struck.

Bodies fell to the floor all around the room, and the four people still conscious cautiously raised their heads and peered around.

I hurried over to Hades, grabbing his arm and yanking him up to his feet. "Let's go!"

[9]

We raced back to the *Argo*, reaching the ship just as shouts erupted from across the Parc de l'Ariana. Either the stunned guards from the Security Council chamber had remarkable recovery time, or one had roused enough to call in reinforcements and send them after us.

Hades used his holoband to lead us directly to the *Argo*'s loading ramp, and we trailed behind him into the ship, heartbeats hammering as we dragged in lungfuls of air. Fiona and Meg stood off to the side of the loading ramp, eyes opened wide as they watched our calamitous return.

My mom brushed her hair out of her sweaty face and let out a breathy laugh. She leaned forward, planting her hands on her knees, and shook her head. "So much for diplomacy . . ."

Hades rounded on me, anger pulsing from him in waves. "That was completely unnecessary," he said, his voice raised.

I held his stare, collapsing the doru and tucking it into the sheath on my back before activating my regulator to shut out his volatile emotions. "I disagree," I snapped.

"You may have ruined any chance we had for diplomatic

relations with that stunt," he went on, a vein bulging in his forehead.

"Looked to me like you were doing that all on your own." Anger surged within me, rising to meet his. I walked past him to slap my hand against the switch that would manually raise the loading ramp. I planted one hand on my hip and turned to face him, vaguely aware of the others shrinking back as they watched the confrontation. "If I didn't know better, I'd have said this was what you wanted all along—an excuse to abandon this planet and focus on saving the Olympians."

Hades fumed, his nostrils flaring, and he marched toward me.

I raised one eyebrow, not the least bit intimidated.

"I gave you my word I would help the humans," he said, looming over me. "Why do you still doubt me?"

My resolve stumbled, and my hand slipped from my hip. "What would you have had me do?" I asked, my voice softening as my anger dissipated, revealing the true source of my intense response—fear. "Just let them take you?" I searched his icy stare, trying to understand. "They would have tortured you and dissected you and done all kinds of horrible things to you, and I —" I swallowed roughly, shaking my head. Didn't he get that he was one of the people I would do anything to protect? "I couldn't just stand by and let that happen."

Hades seemed to deflate on his next exhale. "I could have reasoned with them," he said, smoothing back the few strands of silver-blond hair that had escaped from the tie at the nape of his neck. "They are frightened, and when humans are frightened, they act irrationally. In time, their rational minds would have taken over. Allowing them the appearance of having the upper hand would have expedited that process."

My hands balled into fists as his words coaxed fresh anger from the dying embers. I threw my head back and growled in frustration, blowing off some steam before lifting my head to glare at him. "You could have shared your plan with me," I said, gritting my teeth. "But you would never do that because you always think you know what's best."

"Because I usually do," he said, his cheek twitching. I would have sworn he was fighting a smile, the smug bastard.

"Not this time." I snapped. "You may have studied humans over the millennia, but I lived among them—as one of them—and there is no bargain you could have made that would have been enough." I took a small step closer, tilting my head back to stare Hades straight in the eye. "They're facing extinction, Hades. Their survival instincts are kicking in. Their rational minds are gone. We don't have time for you to play captive. Everyone on this planet is going to die—human, Olympian, *everyone*—unless we do something about it *now*."

"We could have worked with them," Hades said, holding his ground, though some of the certainty had left his voice, and his statement sounded a lot like a question. "Worked together," he added.

I laugh under my breath and shook my head, looking past my mom and Emi toward the windshield at the front of the ship to watch the people milling around in the park, going about their day. "No," I said. "We could have *let them use us*." I sighed, suddenly exhausted. "They would have used us up until there was nothing left of us."

I made my way up to the front of the ship and gripped the top of my seatback as I watched the armed guards search the grounds. They couldn't see the ship, but it was only a matter of time until one of them stumbled upon it through sheer dumb luck.

"I've already sacrificed myself to save this planet once before," I said, my voice distant, "and it didn't change a damn thing. We're right back where we started." I bowed my head, my grip on the seatback tightening until the color bleached from my knuckles. "I won't let you do the same thing. We do this together, Hades, or we don't do it at all."

Tense silence filled the ship. A hand landed on my shoulder, and I knew without looking that it belonged to my mom.

An alarm blared suddenly, followed by the distinct sound of one of the guards knocking on the outside of the ship.

"I think they've found us," my mom said from beside me, crouching slightly to peer out through the windshield.

Several guards searching nearby areas started heading our way.

My mom glanced over her shoulder at Hades. "Might want to get this thing in the air . . ."

Hades strode forward and slid into his seat in front of the controls. With the flip of a switch, he started the engine, and within seconds, we were in the air, leaving behind four very confused UN guards, blinking in the wind created by our liftoff.

[10]

I sat cross-legged on the floor in the aft of the *Argo*, Meg seated directly in front of me. Cloaked in invisibility, the ship took up the eastern end of the parking lot nearest our mark on the CERN campus, the Atlantea Project building. The stone in Meg's regulator glowed a brilliant amethyst to mine's electric blue, and the channels running the length of our hoplon suits matched the colors of our psychic energy.

Meg's eyes were closed, and her face was a mask of concentration as she focused on our bond and on sensing what I was doing.

With a thought and a focused surge of psychic energy, I activated my hoplon suit's stealth mode, making myself invisible to the naked eye.

The muscles in Meg's face tensed, and the next moment, she too blinked out of sight.

I clapped my hands together, squealing with delight as I dropped out of stealth mode and became visible again. "You did it!" I beamed at the younger psychic as she winked back into sight.

Meg's eyes were alight with excitement, and her grin

mirrored mine. She was a talented psychic warrior but learning to operate the hoplon suit's more advanced features was proving to be a challenge, even for her. It had taken two hours of focus and failed attempts, but finally, she could control the suit's stealth capabilities. Not that the time lost to this lesson mattered all that much.

We had to wait until nightfall to infiltrate the Atlantea Project building anyway, so Meg could assist. Her lethal case of solar urticaria meant she was a nighttime-only operative. And as the only other psychic on our team, she was essential to our success on this mission. Hades had already promised to reverse the genetic marker causing her toxic sunlight allergy as soon as we got the Alpha site up and running, but until then, she had to stay indoors during the daylight hours. It was a massive weakness for such a powerful ally.

"Just remember," I warned her, "maintaining the illusion of invisibility for too long will drain your reserves of psychic energy, so only use it when absolutely necessary. For this mission, as soon as the cameras and the security system are down, drop the illusion. There's a good chance you'll need to save your energy for a battle." I reached for her hand, squeezing her fingers. "We can't fail, tonight. It's do or die."

Meg nodded. "I understand," she said solemnly.

That we wanted the chaos stone was no secret, and the UN had already sent over extra security to guard the building. Heavily armed guards now manned the entrance and patrolled around the building. I could sense their minds—dozens of them, muted by distance but there, nonetheless. Stunning them wouldn't be an option, not with the chaos stone so close. A wayward blast of psychic energy could initiate a catastrophic chain reaction. If we were caught in there, we would need to be careful and a little creative about the way we fought.

Adrenaline surging as I anticipated the coming mission, I stood, then offered a hand to Meg and pulled her up to her feet.

With a faint hum, the ship's loading ramp began to lower, and we both looked toward the growing opening. The sound of footsteps signaled Fiona's approach from further in the ship. Her mind throbbed with excitement, and her surface thoughts told me she couldn't wait to get inside the Atlantea Project building and snoop around.

The CERN complex was like a college campus, with numerous buildings sprawled across a nearly one-square-mile area. The organization mainly focused on particle physics, with buildings devoted to studying this or that aspect of the field, along with seventeen miles of underground tunnels making up the world's largest particle accelerator, but they also dabbled in the computer sciences and were largely responsible for the invention of the World Wide Web. It wasn't hyperbole to say they had changed the world. Or to say that if we didn't steal the world's first truly renewable power source—the chaos stone— their greatest achievement would *end* the world, once and for all.

As the loading ramp lowered, our target came into view. The Atlantea Project building was shaped like a cube, the exterior almost entirely composed of smokey glass. The windows gleamed in the rising moonlight, making the building look like a giant block of obsidian.

The external security measures had been reinforced by UN guards, but the internal security was the real problem. According to Fiona and Meg's research, there wasn't an inch of the interior that wasn't covered by cameras and motion sensors, and each lab within the building had restricted access controlled by biometric-coded key cards, cards that would only work when handled by their designated owners. And to make matters worse, the central lab where we wagered the chaos stone was being held, was rigged to lock down if the security system *or* personnel suspected anything hinky.

I could trick the key cards into working with a little psychic mojo, and I could make the security personnel see whatever I wanted them to see when they looked at us, but if anyone was monitoring the cameras, they would spot us—even Meg and me in stealth mode. Brute force wouldn't help us here. This job required finesse, which wasn't exactly one of my strong suits.

When the loading ramp touched asphalt, my mom boarded the ship, sporting a pristine new lab coat she hadn't been wearing when she'd left fifteen minutes earlier. Whatever labels my mom liked to assign herself—archaeologist, treasure hunter, explorer—there was one label that fit her best: thief. Her contribution to the great chaos stone heist was to steal what we needed to sneak Fiona into the building. Hades might have been the expert when it came to Olympian tech, but Fiona outshone him in every possible way when it came to human technologies. We would need her in there, and while I could alter the perception of others to make them see her differently, I couldn't make her disappear completely. For her to get into the building, she needed a disguise and credentials. And it was my mom's job to get the things we would need to make that happen.

My mom reached for my arm as she passed me, giving me a gentle squeeze, then handed her prize—one of the *almost* infallible key cards—to Fiona. "Like taking candy from a baby," she proclaimed, a wry smile twisting her lips. "Caught him on his way to his car."

I moved closer to Fiona, craning my neck to get a look at the key card. The photo on the front displayed the face of a chubby, balding, olive-skinned man: Dr. Alejandro Castillo, according to the bold text typed below the photo.

"A woman would have been easier," I said, glancing up from the key card to meet my mom's eyes. "Less work to trick their minds into believing the disguise."

Her smile wilted as she shrugged out of the lab coat.

Fiona shook her head. "No, this is perfect," she countered. She accepted the lab coat when my mom handed it to her, slipping first one arm in, then the other. "Dr. Castillo is one of the

Atlantea Project leads." Fiona clipped the key card onto the breast pocket of the lab coat. "He has top-level clearance," she went on. "This badge will give us access to every inch of that place." She pointed to me. "And, he's a little guy—rounder, but not much taller than me, so that ought to help with the illusion."

She pulled out her phone and swiped through some pictures before holding it out to me, showing me a full-body shot of Dr. Castillo standing beside some colleagues. Either they were all giants, or he really was a shorty.

Fiona looked from me to Meg and back. "It'll help, right? At least a little?"

For long seconds, I studied the image of Dr. Castillo, cataloging as many details as possible. Finally, I sighed, mentally preparing for the additional strain this illusion would put on my psychic abilities to alter Fiona's appearance so drastically while maintaining my own relative invisibility. "Alright," I said, "but try to walk like this guy would walk. That'll make the illusion more believable."

Fiona adjusted her lab coat by the lapels, widening her stance and slouching a little. "How's this?"

I frowned, assessing her posture and briefly overlaying a rough illusion of Dr. Castillo in her place. "Not bad," I admitted. "And if you can help it, don't talk. I don't know what his voice sounds like, so the best I can do is guess. If those guards know him . . ."

"No talking," Fiona said with a nod. "Got it."

The others had gathered around us in the back of the ship as we discussed the disguise. Now that my mom was back and we had what we needed, it was go time.

I looked around, scanning the faces of all the people I loved. I *had* to pull this off—for them and their world. I never knew my homeworld, thanks to the Tsakali, but I'd be damned if I let my mom, Raiden, and the others lose theirs.

Each of them nodded as my eyes met theirs. Whatever happened, we were in this together.

I looked at Hades last. "If something goes wrong in there, you get them out of here."

He stared at me for a long moment. "I believe I speak for everyone when I say that we will not abandon you."

A quick glance at Raiden and his set jaw, at my mom and her quirked eyebrow, at Emi and her crossed arms, told me it was hopeless to argue.

I blew out a breath. "Great. No pressure."

Raiden pushed through the gap between my mom and Emi and wrapped his arms around me, holding me tight against him. His concern seeped into me, but so did his certainty that I would succeed. He tucked my head under his chin and held me snug and tight, and I clung to him. For so long, he had been my crutch, my safety net. This was my first big mission without him.

"You got this," Raiden said, his voice a low rumble. "Don't overthink it. In and out, and then we're gone." He gave me one last squeeze, then released me.

I searched his eyes, seeing nothing but his utter conviction that I could do this—without him. Since the merging of my past and present selves, I had been thinking of Raiden as a reminder of how weak I had let myself become in this lifetime. But I could see now that I had been wrong. He believed in me, had always believed in me, far more than I did. Back when I was just Cora, his belief in me had given me the confidence I had needed to venture out into the world and save my mom. Hades was right: my loved ones weren't a weakness at all. They made me stronger, each in their own way.

Holding my head high, I turned my back to Raiden and started down the loading ramp, Meg and Fiona falling in step behind me. I paused at the foot of the ramp, safe within the veil of the ship's cloak, taking a moment to activate my hoplon suit's stealth mode. Through our bond, I could sense Meg doing the same.

I glanced over my shoulder at Fiona, concentrating on her appearance. In a blink, a far more detailed illusion of Dr. Castillo than I had created earlier replaced her.

"It's done," I told her. "Let's get moving. The longer we have Dr. Castillo's key card, the more likely he is to notice it's missing."

Meg and I waited for Fiona to take the lead, then flanked her as we started across the parking lot toward the boxy building looming ahead. We passed several pairs of patrolling guards, but they must have recognized Fiona's disguise as the man who had left the building just a short time ago because all they did was nod and continue on their way.

The guards at the door watched Fiona as she held her key card up to the reader. I stared at the key card, sending the thinnest threads of psychic energy into the deceptively complex device to trick its internal mechanism into activating. The card reader beeped a cheerful note, and the yellow light at the top of the reader blinked to green. The door lock disengaged with a click, and the guard to the right of the door pulled it open.

Fiona nodded to the guard as she entered the building, Meg and I close on her heels.

Not quite a dozen paces into the lobby, our way was blocked by a standing metal detector and a security desk manned by another guard—this one looking like he wasn't on loan from the UN and actually belonged here, according to the CERN logo embroidered over his name on his breast pocket.

Meg and I silently slipped around the metal detector while Fiona stopped at the desk and flashed her key card to the guard.

"Forget something, Dr. Castillo?" the guard asked, his voice carrying a heavy French accent. He scanned the key card with a hand-held card reader. From the guard's mind, I sensed this happened often with Dr. Castillo.

Breath held, I turned to watch the interaction between Fiona and the guard. I formed a telepathic connection with Fiona's mind and reminded her not to speak.

Looking slightly uncomfortable, Fiona laughed silently and shrugged one shoulder.

"Try to be quick," the guard told Fiona. "We're expecting some trouble tonight."

Fiona made a good show of looking alarmed and nodded hurriedly. She rushed through the metal detector, and I followed her down the main hallway toward a set of reinforced double doors. The sign over the doors read *LABORATORY 1.*

Meg split off into a side hallway, heading for the security hub to disable the cameras.

With my help, Fiona used the key card to unlock the double doors. She pushed her way through the unlocked doors, lingering in the doorway to let me pass.

The room beyond was dome-shaped and cavernous, and remarkably barren. The curved walls were white with criss-crossing silver lines forming a diamond pattern, and the only objects in the lab were a control station set off to one side and a column in the absolute center of the space. The column was constructed of some shiny, silver metal, broken at chest-height by a foot-long gap. A ball of silver light no larger than my fist hovered in the gap, twisting and writhing like it was alive, held in place by an electromagnetic field.

"There it is," I murmured, taking a hesitant step closer to the chaos stone.

I had never actually seen a chaos stone in person before. The chaos stone that had powered the *Tartarus* had burned out from too frequent use of the FTL drive during the journey to Earth from Olympus, leaving us with shattered fragments of the once-powerful stone. The fragments themselves had retained enough potency to power the gephyra, but just barely.

Fiona slowly approached the hovering mass of near-endless

power. "It's so beautiful," she said, her voice distant. She stopped just out of arm's reach of the column and crouched to get a closer look. "I had no idea it would be so beautiful."

I stared past her, equally mesmerized by the chaos stone.

The lights flickered, shaking me out of my reverie, and through my bond with Meg, I could sense that the security system had been disabled. Not only did we not have to worry about cameras and motion sensors anymore, but the lockdown was no longer an issue.

Exhaling in relief, I dropped out of stealth mode and let go of the illusion masking Fiona's appearance. "Fio," I said, approaching her position near the column displaying the chaos stone, "we're clear. Get to work on the EM field." When she didn't respond, I nudged her arm.

Fiona blinked at me. "Sorry. What did you say?"

"Security's down," I told her and pointed to the control station with my chin. "You're up."

She would need to disable the electromagnetic field holding the chaos stone in place before I could move it. EM fields were like kryptonite to psychics, blocking our powers, or nullifying them completely when used on a grand enough scale. The Tsakali had exploited that weakness to great effect during the final strike that drove my people from Olympus.

"Oh," Fiona said, blinking dazedly. "Right." She shot one last yearning glance at the chaos stone, then spun around and jogged over to the control station. When she reached the oversized computer, she immediately set to work hacking into the system, her fingers flying over the keyboard.

I turned back to the chaos stone and took a step closer, cocking my head to the side as I studied the glowing, writhing mass. It was smaller than I had thought it would be but no less impressive. I waited a few minutes, then raised my hands and attempted to wrap the chaos stone in a cocoon of psychic energy, but the EM field was still in place, and as I had expected, the waves of electric-blue energy fizzled out of existence inches from the chaos stone.

I glanced over my shoulder at Fiona. She had stopped typing and was staring down at a sheet of paper she held in her hand. "Fio?" I turned to face her fully, my hands settling on my hips. "Is there a problem?"

Fiona continued to stare down at the piece of paper, her brow furrowing. "I don't know," she said. "Maybe." She looked up, her eyes meeting mine. "This memo is signed by Henry Magnusson."

"*What*?" I blurted, rushing over to see the damning signature for myself. I rounded the desk and took the memo from Fiona, skimming over the bulk of the writing until my eyes locked on the name typed at the bottom. "No," I breathed, shaking my head. "It's not possible."

I could feel Fiona's stare burning into the side of my face. "What does it mean?"

It meant the Custodes Veritatis was involved in the Atlantea Project.

Again, I shook my head. The Custodes Veritatis had been founded by Hades some three thousand years ago. He had trusted the group with the history of our people. With the cause of our downfall. Because of him, they had known about chaos stones and orichalcum, the element from which chaos stones were made. They had known about the Tsakali's endless drive to possess any and all sources of the unique renewable energy known as chaos. There was no way the Order could have been involved in the Atlantea Project and *not* been aware of the consequences.

I licked my lips, horrified by the implications. "It means," I said, my voice haunted, "that Henry called the Tsakali here."

[11]

I stared at the chaos stone, my thoughts spinning as I attempted to puzzle out the mystery of Henry's involvement in the Atlantea Project. There was no other explanation—the Custodes Veritatis had to have been the driving force behind the project. They must have recognized the composition of the meteor for what it was as soon as it was fished out of the Bering Sea, orichalcum, and they must have encouraged CERN scientists to explore ways that the novel element could be used as a power source.

I glanced over my shoulder, watching Fiona type furiously at the control station near the edge of the lab for a moment, then returned my attention to the chaos stone. The second the EM field was down, we were out of here.

The thing that really confused me about the Order's involvement in the Atlantea Project was why they would push for the creation of something so dangerous. Something Henry had to have known was dangerous. I hadn't read through the entirety of the *Liber Veritatis*, the book that functioned as the abridged compendium of all the Order's knowledge and history, but I had read enough to know that the Order's leaders were aware of the general cause of the fall of our people—the

Tsakali and their endless hunger for chaos stones. There had to be something I was missing because I could not, for the life of me, figure out *why* they would purposely risk drawing the Tsakali here.

Suddenly the world seemed to dim, the air becoming uncomfortably fuzzy, and I could no longer sense Fiona behind me or even Meg's presence hovering on the edges of my mind. For the first time since it had been established, our bond was gone. The absence was as devastating as if I'd lost a limb.

"What the hell?" Fiona grumbled.

"No, no, no . . ." I glanced down at my regulator, not surprised to see that the stone didn't glow at all—no electric blue, no amber, nothing but a clear, colorless gemstone. The channels running the length of my hoplon suite had gone dark as well. I drew my doru but couldn't extend the staff to its full length without access to my internal reserves of psychic energy. Only one thing could affect my psychic powers like this—being surrounded by an electromagnetic field.

I spun around. "Fiona, please tell me you did something to the EM field . . ."

Fiona paused her forceful punching of the same key over and over to look at me. Her lips were pressed together in a thin, bloodless line that told me I wasn't the only one screwed over by the new, larger EM field. "The damn thing froze, and then it just shut off," she said, her voice rising in pitch with each successive word.

The double doors swung inward, and Fiona ducked down behind the control station as at least a dozen armed soldiers filed into the lab, fanning out along the curved wall. These were no UN guards; these were Custodes Veritatis soldiers, and every single one held an assault rifle that was aimed at me.

I raised my hands over my head, my retracted doru held in a tight grip. Hatred narrowed my eyes to a glare as one final person strolled into the lab, his tailored charcoal suit standing in stark contrast to his soldiers' armored black tactical gear. Henry Magnusson had joined the party.

I turned all my attention on the douchebag threatening not only the survival of my people but of his own people, as well.

Henry peered around the room, taking in the positions of all his soldiers, and then his stare landed on me, catching me red-handed by the chaos stone. He moved closer, each of his steps echoing around the too-still room but stopped well out of reach. His lips curved into a cruel, closed-mouth smile. "Hello again, ancient one."

I ground my molars together, fighting the urge to curse at him as my fingers itched to close around his throat. "What did you do?" I ground out.

Henry clasped his hands behind his back. "What needed to be done," he said, his lilting Scandinavian accent grating on my nerves. "If you and your people don't want to share your technology, we'll find someone else who will."

"We never said we wouldn't share our technology," I said, struggling to keep my voice calm and even. "We said we wouldn't hand over what remains of our people."

"Tomato, tom*a*to," Henry said, his eyes sparkling with a challenge. "The Security Council and I are more than willing to negotiate with Hades if he finds himself in a more cooperative mood. If not . . ." Henry shrugged one shoulder. "There are other ways to get what we need."

"You don't *need* alien technology," I scoffed. "Besides, the Tsakali aren't going to share theirs with you anyway, you moron. They're going to *destroy* you." I gestured to the chaos stone behind me with a violent jerk of my free hand. "You rang the dinner bell. No turning back now."

A wicked grin curved Henry's thin lips. "Didn't you ever wonder why the Tsakali were so hellbent on destroying the Olympians?"

"They want our chaos stones," I said, my voice cold. "They

need them to survive, and they don't know how to make them themselves."

Henry narrowed his eyes and raised one hand, tapping his index finger against his lips. "Ah," he mused, "but if that were true wouldn't it have made more sense for the Tsakali to bargain with the Olympians instead of destroying them? To strike a deal wherein Olympus was turned into a chaos stone factory? To enslave their enemy into serving their needs?"

I was quiet for a long moment as my mind worked through the possible implications of his questions. "The Tsakali don't make deals," I told him. "All they care about is consuming. Possessing. Destroying."

"They don't make deals at all?" Henry asked, cocking his head to the side. The amusement sparkling in his eyes told me I was playing right into his hand.

I clenched my jaw.

"Or do they only not make deals with Olympians?" Henry continued, frowning. His exaggerated expression told me not only that he found this question immensely fascinating, but that he already knew the answer. "Ask Hades about it, why don't you?"

He turned and started slowly pacing around the lab, stopping when he reached the opposite side of the column holding the suspended chaos stone. "It is truly wondrous, is it not?" he asked, gazing at the writhing, glowing mass of energy. "Too bad you can't get to it. How does it feel to be powerless, like the rest of us?" His focus shifted past the chaos stone to me. "We embedded an EM field generator into the walls just for you, you know. What an honor."

I let out a hollow, bitter laugh. "You think stripping me of my psychic abilities makes me powerless?" I smirked. "That's adorable."

Without warning, I chucked my doru at a soldier standing across the lab, momentarily directing the attention of the room away from me, then dove for the nearest soldier, using his body as a shield when the others opened fire on me. The hoplon suit would still protect me from the brunt of the force of the bullets, but without psychic energy reinforcing the armored fabric, it was no longer impenetrable. I felt a twinge of guilt for taking the soldier's life, but he had chosen this path. Besides, what was one life when compared to the fate of everyone, Earth-born and Olympian, residing on this planet?

The sound of all the gunfire in the enclosed space was deafening, but my human shield proved most effective. I took out five more soldiers with his rifle, and two fell victim to friendly fire, before one tackled me into the wall. The borrowed assault rifle flew from my hands and slid across the floor, well out of reach. The endless gunfire had stopped, and the four remaining soldiers were taking a more cautious, strategic approach to subduing me.

I grappled with the soldier who had tackled me, my main focus keeping his body between me and the remaining rifles, or I would have had him disarmed and disabled in a matter of seconds, adrenaline making up for whatever I still lacked in stamina and strength. I managed to drag the soldier up to his feet and back myself against the wall, holding him in front of me with the length of his assault rifle pressed across his throat, cutting off his air supply. Another soldier guarded Henry with his body on the far side of the central column, another slowly snuck closer to me along the wall, and the last—

I shot a panicked look around the room. I had lost track of the fourth remaining soldier.

She popped up from behind the control station, dragging a clawing and kicking Fiona with her. The soldier drew her sidearm and pressed it against Fiona's temple, and my friend instantly fell still.

I stared at the pair, breathing hard as the struggles of the soldier in my arms weakened. "Leave her alone," I demanded.

"Such weakness," Henry said, tutting. "And such predictabil-ity." He strode out from behind the column and the soldier protecting him. "Surrender, or the girl dies."

I looked from Henry to Fiona and back. And then I released my hold on the assault rifle and let the soldier drop to his knees in front of me, retching and gasping for breath. Completely unarmed, I raised my hands over my head and stepped over the soldier on the floor. The sneaking soldier straightened and pulled a zip tie out from one of the many pockets in her pants, and I lowered my arms, pressing my wrists together behind my back and turning away from her. After the first zip tie was secured, she added two more for good measure.

"There now," Henry said, wandering closer, exuding haughty pleasantness. "That wasn't so hard, was it?" He stopped just out of arm's reach. I still could have taken him out, but not without risking Fiona's life, and that was something I wasn't willing to do.

I glared at Henry, imagining wrapping my legs around his head and snapping his neck with a twisting jerk of my body.

Henry gestured to the double doors and raised his eyebrows in invitation. "Shall we?"

The woman who had secured my restraints took hold of my elbow and pushed me toward the doors. The soldier detaining Fiona had shifted her sidearm to Fiona's back in preparation for following us out.

"Sorry," Fiona mouthed as I passed her.

I shook my head, flashing her a weak smile. This wasn't over. There was still a way. There was still Meg.

As soon as I passed through the double doors, the fuzzy quality to the air vanished, and the channels running the length of my hoplon suit flared amber. My regulator, too, was alight with a subtle amber glow, and Meg's presence flared to life in my mind. My psychic gifts were suppressed, but at least they were there. It was a far cry better than the psychic void created by the EM field.

Stay hidden, I told Meg, not that she needed the direction. I could sense her lurking around the corner of the hallway, hiding under an illusion of invisibility.

The soldier restraining me guided me up the hallway, around the security terminal, and back out into the lobby, the others following behind us. When we emerged through the main door to the outside, she pulled me off to the side of the walkway to wait for Henry, giving me a chance to take in the altered scene surrounding the Atlantea Project.

A veritable army of Order soldiers spread out around the building, and a tank idled on the edge of the parking lot, the gun aimed at the building's main door. I watched as the gun slowly adjusted to the right, following me.

Fiona and her detainer exited next, followed by the remaining two soldiers who had survived the encounter in the lab, the man I had nearly choked to death with his own rifle looking the worse for wear. Henry emerged last, his expression all smug satisfaction.

My lip curled in a silent snarl, and I pulled at my restraints, wanting nothing more than to claw my nails across his face.

A loud *thwump* snapped my attention out to the parking lot. A moment later, the tank exploded, sending the soldiers who had been stationed nearest the war machine flying and forcing those around me to the ground. I felt the concussion, but thanks to my hoplon suit, it didn't knock me down. My ears rang from the massive *boom* though, and I blinked to clear the smoke and dust from my eyes as debris rained down all around me.

Heartbeats later, when the smoke cleared, I spotted my mom out in the parking lot, about halfway between the remains of the demolished tank and our cloaked ship. She was down on one knee, reloading an honest-to-god rocket launcher, channeling her inner Sarah Connor. I had never been happier to see her in my life.

Raiden and Emi stood off to one side of my mom, Hades to the other. They were armed to the teeth with an array of human and Olympian weapons, ranging from assault rifles to laser pistols. Every single weapon was trained on Henry, who was just climbing to his feet after being knocked down by the blast.

"Let them go, Henry," my mom said as she finished reloading the rocket launcher and aimed the devastating weapon at her archnemesis. "Maybe your people could take out one or two of us, but you won't get us all before we get you."

Taking advantage of the attention being off me, for the moment, I gritted my teeth and wrenched my arms backward and up, dislocating my left shoulder. I hissed in a breath, pushing through the searing pain, and pulled my zip-tied wrists over my head. Thankfully, my shoulder joint popped back into place as soon as my arms were in front of me. Hastily, I deactivated my regulator, and my psychic gifts flared to life.

"Sir!" the soldier who had restrained me cried out, but she was too late.

With a single, focused thought, I raised my bound wrists, wincing at the sharp pain in my injured shoulder, and jerked my hands closer to me, seizing all the weapons held by Order soldiers and ripping them from their grasps. My shoulder screamed in pain, but I couldn't stop. I wouldn't, not until we were free and the chaos stone was ours. A hoarse scream burst from my chest as I dug deep into my reserves of psychic energy and tore the weapons apart.

Stunned stares followed me as I hurried over to Fiona, who was still huddled on the ground, and helped her up to her feet. Huddled together, we followed the path leading from the building to the parking lot, and not a single Order soldier tried to stop us.

"You can kill us all," Henry called after us, "but we will

never drop the EM field, and you'll never get your precious chaos stone." I could practically hear the spittle flying from his lips.

"Keep them distracted," I told my mom when we reached her and the others.

My mom nodded, the corner of her mouth lifting. She sucked in a breath to hurtle taunts Henry's way, feeding fuel into his manic tirade.

Raiden pulled a combat knife from the sheath strapped to his thigh and cut through the ties on my wrist. "How's your shoulder?"

"I'll heal," I said, compartmentalizing the pain.

I crouched down, planting my right hand on the asphalt and closing my eyes, seeking out the lines of electricity feeding power into the Atlantea Project building. Once I found them, I sought out the backup generators in the basement level. Digging deep, I severed the lines that connected the building to all its power sources. The EM field couldn't operate without power.

Psychic energy surged out of me, draining me completely, and I fell forward onto my hands and knees, my head hanging. My shoulder screamed in pain.

A supportive arm curved around my middle, keeping me from collapsing completely. Raiden. A tiny smile curved my lips. He was always there when I needed him most.

I opened my eyes and raised my head just in time to see Meg walk out of the building behind Henry, the chaos stone hovering between her outstretched hands in front of her.

Henry's mouth fell open, and he stumbled out of the way as Meg passed him.

I grinned, drawing in a ragged breath. "Checkmate, asshole."

[12]

We hurried back to the *Argo* and raised the loading ramp as soon as everyone was inside the ship. Injured arm tucked close to my body, I activated my regulator, suppressing my psychic senses, and watched the chaos unfolding in front of the Atlantea Project building until the opening at the back of the ship was too small to see much of anything. My last view of Henry was of him gesturing wildly and shouting at the soldiers around him.

Smiling to myself, I turned away from the loading ramp. Hushed but expectant silence filled the space. My mom, Raiden, Emi, and Fiona stood off to the left, huddled together as they watched Hades and Meg on the opposite side of the ship. Hades was holding open a one-foot square orichalcum containment cube while Meg carefully lowered the volatile chaos stone into the compartment. The cube was made for this specific purpose, the inner lining emitting a self-contained EM field that would cradle the chaos stone in a safe environment during transport.

Hades closed the lid on the containment cube, and it let out a hiss of air as it sealed. He placed the cube in a storage compartment under the floor, sent a quick glance my way, then headed up to the seats at the front and reclaimed his place at the helm. I followed him but didn't sit; instead, I leaned as far forward as possible without smooshing my face against the windshield to watch more of the scene outside.

Within a matter of seconds, we were in the air, and I stared out the window until the Atlantea Project building was so small that it looked like a toy and the individual people were impossible to see.

At the sound of laughter, light and bubbly, I turned around, leaning my hip against the side of the empty seat.

Fiona slapped a hand over her mouth, but the laughter burst out anyway. "I'm sorry!" she exclaimed, doubling over, one arm hugging her middle, the other propped against the side of the ship.

My mom's lips twitched, and a chuckle tickled my chest. Raiden grinned like a goofball, Meg's shoulders shook with silent laughter, and even serious, stoic Emi wore a tight-lipped smile. Hades glanced over his shoulder, his expression telling me he thought we were all nuts.

"We're alive!" Fiona gasped between bouts of uncontrollable laughter. She snorted, waving a hand in front of her as she tried to catch her breath, then collapsed onto the bench seat lining the left side of the ship. "I almost can't believe it," she said once her laughter had died down. She wiped under her eyes, looking my way. "I thought for sure we were goners when you surrendered . . ."

I crossed the ship and sank onto the bench seat to sit beside her. I shook my head, laughing under my breath. It had been close. Once I had seen the army Henry had gathered, I had feared we were done for, too.

My mom leaned back against the opposite side of the ship, crossing her arms over her chest. "What was Henry doing there, anyway? It was almost like he had a stake in the game—beyond you and Hades, I mean."

I sighed and rested my head back against the ship wall. In all the excitement, I had forgotten about Fiona's discovery. "The Order's involved in the Atlantea Project," I shared. "Fiona found—"

"This," Fiona said, pulling a folded-up sheet of paper from the front pocket of her jeans and holding it out in front of her, offering it to my mom.

My mom crossed to our side of the ship and took the folded paper, then sat down beside Fiona. She unfolded the memo and skimmed the writing, her eyes narrowing to slits when she reached the bottom of the page. "Henry . . ." The name came out as a low growl passing through her lips. She handed the memo to Emi, standing nearby, then looked at me.

"Henry knew creating a chaos stone could draw the Tsakali's notice," I explained as Emi and Raiden skimmed the note together. "He *wanted* it to draw their notice."

I relayed all I had learned during the encounter with Henry in the lab—that he was willing to play a deadly game of chicken with the *whole world* in order to get his hands on all that remained of the Olympians here on Earth, including the Olympians themselves. When I was finished, a stunned silence settled over the group.

My attention drifted to the front of the ship, to Hades. I stared at the back of his head, wanting to ask him if there was any merit to the things Henry had implied about the Tsakali and our people. Was there more to the story? Had our people done something to the Tsakali to draw their eternal wrath?

I had left that part out of my recap, and either Fiona didn't notice, or she was smart enough to leave it to me to approach Hades about it later. Henry Magnusson was a devious, manipulative man, but if there was any merit to the things he had implied—if there was any chance that the Tsakali weren't mindless killers, but rather vengeful hunters with a taste for Olympian blood—then Earth and humanity had a much better chance at surviving their arrival. *If* there was any merit to what Henry had implied. It was a big *if*.

"Well," Emi began, handing the memo back to my mom who folded it up and tucked it into a pocket. "I suppose it doesn't really matter why the chaos stone was created, just that it *was* created and now we have to deal with the consequences."

I nodded. Good old Emi, ever the practical one.

My mom stood and pulled Emi over to the other side of the ship where the two bent their heads together, no doubt discussing Henry and his misguided motivations.

Raiden sat down beside me on the bench as a wave of exhaustion flooded through me, and I rested my head on his shoulder. I'd tiptoed along a dangerous threshold by expending so much psychic energy, and now that the fight was over and the adrenaline had drained from my system, I was ready to crash. It was a good, cautionary reminder of how my last life had ended. I'd pushed myself too hard, expended too much psychic energy, and something inside me had broken. I couldn't let that happen again, not while the people I loved were in such grave danger.

"Thanks for saving me," I told Raiden. "Again."

He wrapped his arm around my shoulders, laughter a low rumble in his chest. "Much as I'd like to take credit, the ambush was all your mom's idea. As soon as she saw that dickbag marching toward the building . . ."

I could only imagine what had happened next, could only relish the knowledge that my mom had stolen a rocket launcher from the enemy soldiers. She was nothing if not resourceful. I watched her from across the ship, deep in her discussion with Emi, in awe of her ability to pull off the seemingly impossible. And she was just a regular old human with no psychic powers to fall back on. This was my eighteenth cycle—my eighteenth lifetime—but my first with a flesh-and-blood mother. She was amazing, and I felt incredibly lucky that she had chosen to be my mom. Maybe she wouldn't win any mother of the year awards, but she was one hell of a role model.

Meg crossed in front of my mom and Emi, heading toward the front of the ship, and I followed her with my eyes. She sat in the empty seat beside Hades, and the two started quietly speaking to one another. Through my bond with Meg, I could sense the direction of their conversation—reversing Meg's condition. Hades had committed to dedicating his full attention to the process as soon as we arrived at the Alpha site and had plugged in the chaos stone, powering up the long-abandoned city. As I eavesdropped on their conversation, my eyelids grew heavy.

Before I knew it, Raiden was shaking me with the arm he had wrapped around my shoulders. "Cora," he murmured, "wake up."

I blinked my eyes open, my jaw cracking as I yawned. "I fell asleep," I said as I looked around without raising my head from Raiden's shoulder. My eyelids felt gritty, my head groggy.

Fiona had replaced Meg in the second seat at the front of the ship. My mom stood behind her seat, her hands gripping the top of the seatback, and Meg stood beside my mom, both ducking down to peer out through the windshield. Emi sat further down on the bench seat, a notepad on her lap as she meticulously drew up a bulleted list.

My attention returned to Raiden. "How long have I been out?"

A thoughtful frown turned down the corners of his mouth. "An hour, maybe?" He shrugged, his eyes skimming up toward the top of the ship's hull. "This thing is fast. Switzerland to Antarctica in a little over an hour . . ." He whistled, shaking his head.

"You mean—" I sat up straighter, dislodging his arm, suddenly much more awake. "We're here?"

"We're getting close," he corrected. He pointed toward the

front of the ship with his chin. "Hades thought you'd be interested in watching our approach."

"Hades thought right," I said, my heart beating faster.

The Alpha site had been my home for sixteen cycles, including my last, which had ended in a blaze of glory. I stood and hurried to the front of the ship, more excited than I had expected to be returning to the ice-bound city.

I planted my feet behind Hades' seat and rested my forearms on the top of his seatback as I bent down slightly to get the best view possible. The view through the windshield was divided in half by the blue of the sky and the white of the ice covering the land below.

Hades craned his neck to glance back at me. "Ready to go home?"

I nodded vehemently, not tearing my stare from the windshield.

Hades shifted the controls, and the ship glided lower, closing the distance between us and the frozen ground with frightening speed. We slowed at what felt like the last possible second, and the *Argo* hovered a few feet over the ice.

Hades flipped a switch on the control panel, and the ship shook momentarily as a holoscreen appeared in front of him. The screen provided a secondary view, showing us the ice directly below the ship. Hades raised his hand and tapped a spot on the holoscreen, locking on a target.

A faint humming sound filled my ears, and seconds later, a bright orange laser beam struck the ice at an angle. The ice steamed as it melted around the beam, forming a perfect tunnel through the frozen barrier.

"I haven't been back here for nearly fifteen hundred years," Hades said, watching the beam cut through the ice. "Not since I was scavenging parts to repair the Omega site." Again, he glanced back at me. "It's not the same as it once was," he warned. "Prepare yourself."

The border around the holoscreen flashed red, and a second later, the orange beam cut through the final frozen barrier separating us from the ancient city buried deep below the ice and winked out. Hades flipped the switch on the control panel back to its original position, and the holoscreen disappeared. The ship jarred again as the laser generator retracted into the hull.

I held my breath as Hades guided the *Argo* down through the ice tunnel, darkness triggering the ship's external lights, and soon enough, we emerged into an enormous frozen cavern filled with endless columns of ice, glistening where the light from the ship touched.

The breath escaped from my lungs and my mouth fell open as I realized we weren't in a cavern at all, but the Alpha site, and the frozen columns were actually buildings encased in ice. It was almost unrecognizable as the city I had once known so well. It was like the whole city had been turned into ice and had been slowly melting over the thousands of years since our people abandoned it.

Hades landed the *Argo* on the ground near the base of one of the ice-shrouded buildings. It took me a moment to recognize the building as the central tower. My confusion wasn't all that surprising, considering the "ground" on which we had landed was actually located near the tower's mid-point, with dozens of floors buried beneath the ice. Of course, Hades would start here. The central tower was the heart of the city, and it would provide us the most direct access to the underground mainframe, controlling the entire city's infrastructure, including the power source.

With a flip of that same switch on the control panel as before, Hades initiated the laser generator and the holoscreen appeared once more. This time, he angled the beam projector forward instead of downward. The orange laser beam flared to life in front of the ship and started melting a hole through the ice encasing the central tower. As soon as the holoscreen flashed red, warning us it was almost through the ice, Hades flipped the switch to shut down the laser generator.

"You should probably take over," Hades said, glancing back at me. "If you're up for it. I'd rather not blow out the entire floor." The corner of his mouth tensed, and he leaned forward, peering up toward the top of the tower, which had been consumed by the ceiling of the ice cavern. "We need this building intact."

I knew exactly what he meant. The central tower wasn't just a building; it had been constructed to project an energy field out from the spire at its tip, forming an energy dome that would hold the surrounding ice at bay. If we accidentally destroyed the tower by severing it through the middle, we would never be able to push back the encroaching ice and restore the city to its former glory, and it would remain this frozen wasteland.

Hades punched a button on the control panel, and the ship shuddered as the loading ramp slowly lowered.

I turned and made my way to the back of the ship. As soon as the ramp touched the ice, I started my descent. And for the first time in twelve thousand years, I returned home.

[13]

Retracting my doru, I tucked the weapon back into the sheath on my back and created a ball of glowing energy on my outstretched palm as I led the way through the hole I had just cut through a window in the side of the central tower. I paused just inside the opening and scanned the distinctly administrative space, the electric-blue glow from my energy ball casting eerie shadows. As I looked around, I moved out of the way to let the others through.

Hades entered first, carrying the chaos stone in its orichalcum containment cube, his holoband emitting a strong, white light to illuminate the way for him. The others followed him in through the hole, flashlights in hand, staying close to one another as they looked around, studying the alien structure.

"This place is weirdly normal," Fiona commented. "I mean, cubicles—really?"

I glanced at her, watching her inspect the barren metal surface of a partitioned desk. I wasn't surprised by her reaction. The admin levels of the central tower really did bear a striking resemblance to the interior of the standard modern human office building. It hardly looked *alien*, especially not in comparison to the Omega site, which was Fiona's only frame of reference.

Our entry into the city couldn't have impressed her much, either. To anyone who had never been here before, it would have been nearly impossible to see the mounds and columns of ice for what they really were—the buildings and towers of an ancient Olympian city.

I smiled to myself, thinking Fiona and the others were in for a big surprise. "Just wait," I told Fiona. "Once Hades plugs in the chaos stone and gets this place booted up, you won't be *quite* so disappointed."

Fiona threw me some serious side-eye, her skepticism written all over her face. "You better not be getting my hopes up. I was promised an alien city, but so far all I've seen is an ice cave and some office space. Lame . . ."

I snorted a laugh. "Just trust me, Fio," I said as I started after Hades, who was already halfway across the aforementioned office space.

I picked up the pace, jogging to catch him as he reached the landing to the spiral staircase that wound around and around the glass-paneled lift at the center of the tower. Of course, seeing as the city currently had no functioning power source, the lift was out of order and we had to take the long way down.

Our footsteps on the metal stairs echoed up and down the staircase, sounding too loud in the long-abandoned place. Down, down, down, we descended, passing through seemingly endless floors of cubicles and larger, enclosed offices.

Until, finally, we reached a floor with a ceiling height double that of the higher floors. The staircase was surrounded by a circular corridor with three arched openings, the one nearest the landing being the grandest of the three.

Hades veered off the staircase at the landing and headed for the larger archway, leading us into the cavernous chamber where the gephyra resided. The floor here was polished granite, pearl-white with gray veins, the stone harvested from nearby bedrock. More granite panels lined the walls, cut through by ribs of gleaming silver orichalcum-steel alloy and alternating with huge, floor-to-ceiling windows, their transparency cloaked by the thick sheet of ice coating the exterior of the building. And the gephyra stood at the center of the room, a broad, circular orichalcum platform, ringed by a trio of steps leading down to the granite floor.

"This is it?" my mom said, passing me as she made a beeline for the gephyra. "This is the traveling device?" The others trailed into the chamber, their eyes wandering everywhere.

Raiden followed my mom's path, heading for the gephyra. "This can really transport you to other worlds?" he asked over his shoulder.

I moved off to the side to stand with Hades, letting the others get a good eyeful of the otherworldly device. Honestly, it didn't look like much in its dormant state, but once we powered it up . . . then it would truly be a sight to behold. I couldn't help but recall the first time I had seen it, when Demeter had opened my eyes to the universe.

"The first time I traveled through the gephyra," I told them, "I came here." I snuck a glance at Hades, standing so still beside me. What secrets was he hiding about our people's distant past? "This world was supposed to be our fresh start," I said softly.

But now I wasn't so sure a fresh start was possible for our people. I could have deactivated my regulator and dug through Hades' mind to unearth the truth for myself, but he would have sensed what I was doing, and he wouldn't have appreciated it. He had withheld significant information from me in the past—things I never would have known to look for. I needed to know if he was doing it again, and if he was, why. I *wanted* to trust him, and for that to happen, I needed to give him the chance to volunteer the information on his own. If there was even any information to volunteer. But I *would* give him that chance.

"This is where we'll set up for the time being," Hades said, loud enough for everyone to hear him.

Hades looked at me and lowered his voice. "I'm going to head down to the sublevel to plug the chaos stone in the mainframe."

Fiona turned away from the gephyra's platform and headed our way.

"I may need your help getting in there," Hades went on. "Without power, I'm not sure I'll be able to get through some of the doors."

"You got it," I said with a nod. Besides, the time alone would give me a chance to do a little digging to see if Hades had anything he wanted to share.

Fiona skipped the rest of the way to us, dashing my hopes for a private interrogation. "I'll come with you. There's no way I'm going to miss the chance to see the *mainframe*." She stopped and rubbed her hands together eagerly.

"We'll unload the ship," my mom said, hands on her hips as she scanned the rest of the chamber, her focus finally landing on Hades, then shifting to me. "Unless there's something else we should be doing?"

In my periphery, I saw Hades shake his head and also look at me. I crossed my arms over my chest and stared beyond my mom to the gephyra, a strange combination of anticipation and dread swirling in my gut as I imagined everything the next twenty-four hours might bring. Heading off-world was always a gamble, and after so long, anything could be waiting for us in the lost colonies. There was only one way to find out what, exactly —to go and look for ourselves.

"No," I finally said, dragging my attention back to my mom. "Unloading the *Argo* is perfect. We'll need to unpack all of our bags and repack again with whatever gear we can scrounge up here." I chewed the inside of my cheek, thinking out loud. "I want to hit a couple of other towers before we head out, stock up on some better weapons and gear for everyone . . ."

I turned to the side, staring at the wall of ice blocking one of the massive windows. The tower belonging to the Order of Amazons would be right there, could I see through the frozen glass. Only now it would be empty. A hollow shell of the place it had once been.

I was so distracted by thoughts of the past that I didn't notice my mom's approach until she rested a gentle hand on my shoulder. I looked at her, startled by the contact.

"Are you all right, sweetie?" she asked, compassion crinkling the corners of her eyes. "I can only imagine how strange it is for you to be back here."

A sad smile curved my lips. "Everything is so different." I laughed under my breath and shook my head, slowly scanning the chamber that had been bustling with activity the last time I'd been here. "So empty," I added, my voice sounding distant, even to my own ears.

My mom gave my shoulder a squeeze and offered me a warm smile. "Maybe sometime soon it won't be so empty anymore."

Swallowing hard, I forced myself to nod and returned to staring at the wall of ice blocking the window. I couldn't let myself sink too deeply into the hope that one day soon the Amazon tower would be teeming with my spearsisters once again. Hope could too easily become expectation, and expectation, disappointment.

"Yeah," I breathed. "Maybe."

After one last squeeze of my shoulder, my mom turned away from me and rounded up Raiden, Emi, and Meg, leading them out of the gephyra chamber and back to the spiral staircase. Hades, Fiona, and I followed them, but we headed down the stairs as they climbed back up the way we had come. We wound around and around the glass-encased lift until the staircase ended, and a solid, orichalcum-reinforced door panel blocked the landing beyond the foot of the stairs.

Hades glanced at me over his shoulder and stepped out of the way, waving me forward.

I extinguished my glowing ball of electric-blue energy but didn't even bother drawing my doru. The intensity of the energy blast it would take to bust through the door was likely to damage the hallway beyond, and I didn't think we wanted to risk blocking the passage to the mainframe. And honestly, I wasn't even sure I was capable of creating such a powerful blast right now. Instead of brute force, I stepped forward and pressed my palms against the polished metal door, utilizing a subtler aspect of my psychic abilities.

I closed my eyes and sent my awareness into the door, infusing the mechanisms within with threads of psychic energy. Slowly, holding my breath, I shifted my hands to the left, easing the door panel open. Such a telekinetic feat wouldn't normally have taken so much concentration, but I was still drained from the battle with Henry, and tasks that should have been simple were currently just this side of doable.

After winding through a warren of hallways and forcing our way through two more reinforced doors, we reached the mainframe, a sprawling, labyrinthine space filled with compartments housing dormant machinery. Hades led the way through the maze until we entered a circular clearing. Various machines and devices were scattered around the edge of the space, and a column of stone stood in the center.

Hades made a beeline for the column and set the containment cube on the floor nearby before reaching out to slide a section of the column upward, revealing an opening the length of my forearm. Within sat the city's power core, about the size of a football and covered in a thick layer of squat, greenish crystals.

I moved closer, Fiona trailing behind me, and we both crouched down to get a closer look at the clearly damaged ancient battery. "What happened to it?" I asked, tilting my head to the side. This was the first real hint that time had damaged the city, beyond the slow invasion of the polar ice.

"It looks corroded," Fiona commented.

"Indeed, it is," Hades confirmed. "The humidity caused an internal malfunction within the power core. Regular maintenance would have prevented it, but . . ." Hades sighed, reaching into the opening and grasping either side of the power core. "It happened while I was asleep, and by the time I returned to check on things, the entire Alpha site was too far gone to do anything." With a grunt and a jerk, he pulled the core free, squatting to set it on the floor near the containment cube. "But now, we have a chaos stone, and we'll never have this issue again."

He opened the lid of the containment cube and lifted it up, turning toward me. "Would you do the honors?" He glanced off to the side of the space. "Otherwise I need to get the tongs."

I held out my hands, palms up, and drew on my reserves of psychic energy, coating my hands in a sizzling, electric-blue haze. I nodded to Hades, letting him know I was ready.

Hades gently tilted the cube toward me, until the glowing, writhing chaos stone fell out, hovering an inch above my waiting hands. "All you need to do is place it in the empty receptacle," he said, looking at the opening in the column.

I swallowed, nodding again. Holding my breath, I carried the chaos stone closer to the column, my movements slow and precise. I reached my hands into the opening, then looked at Hades. "Just let it go?"

Hades nodded. "Just let it go."

Exhaling slowly, I shifted my hands out from under the chaos stone. Once my hands were free of the opening, I released my psychic hold on the stone. It dropped into the receptacle, and suddenly, the entire column flared with light. The air hummed around us as the machinery and control panels throughout the vast mainframe powered up.

Hades made his way over to a squat, round machine that reminded me of an old stone well. He started pressing buttons set into the outer rim of the device.

Fiona, eyes opened wide to take it all in, followed him. "What's that?" she asked.

"Power core generator," Hades said, pushing a couple more buttons, then adjusting a dial. "We'll be able to construct a replacement for the Omega site."

Fiona's brow furrowed as she watched Hades' hands, and she raised her eyes to his face. "But I thought that was why we were heading off-world—to find parts to repair the power core in the Omega site?"

I watched their conversation from afar, noticing how Hades was studiously not looking at Fiona. Or at me.

"There are other parts we need to repair the Omega site," Hades said, his focus on the power core generator a little too intent.

Interest piqued, I skimmed the surface of his mind, knowing he wouldn't sense such a gentle touch.

"Parts I can't manufacture here," Hades added, glancing over at me, lurking near the column.

He was lying. And I could sense that he knew that *I* knew he was lying.

Giving up the pretense of staying out of his mind, I delved deeper, until his plan became clear to me. We weren't heading off-world to find parts to fix anything in the Omega site. We would be searching for a hail Mary—a ship that could transport all the Olympian consciousness orbs and preserved embryos held in the Omega site to some new world, along with as many humans as could fit. Because Hades didn't believe there was any way to save this planet. He hadn't shared his true mission with me because he had feared I wouldn't agree to it, that I wouldn't help him gain control of the chaos stone. And he refused to let my stubborn love of this planet bring about the final downfall of our people.

I closed my eyes and shook my head, equally angry and ashamed. Because Hades was probably right. I wouldn't have agreed. And in so doing, I likely would have doomed us all.

I stood on the balcony at the top of the central tower, rested and rejuvenated, surveying the Alpha site. While I had slept, the softly glowing energy dome formed by the spire rising far above my head had pushed back the long encroaching ice to the edges of the settlement's central island and was slowly working its way outward. I was surrounded by gleaming silver and white towers constructed with the swooping angles, arches, and spires distinct to Olympian architecture.

Soon, the canal encircling the central island would be visible and would once again flow with water, generating enough power to run many of the city's surface operations. After that, the industrial land ring would be unveiled, connected to the central island by graceful bridges, followed by the middle canal, then the agricultural land ring and the outer canal.

The parts of the city that had been exposed looked exactly the same as I remembered them, almost like I had never left. But this place *felt* foreign and unfamiliar. When I had been here last, the city had been teeming with life—with Olympians, natural-born and engineered. Now, it was empty. Hollow. Dead.

I leaned on the railing and closed my eyes, imagining the city as it had been so long ago. I recalled the streams of engineered Olympians moving around the city, those who had been created on the *Tartarus*, like me, rather than born back on Olympus before the Tsakali infected our people with the nano-virus that irrevocably tainted our genome and rendered us permanently infertile.

We barely survived the war with the Tsakali. We had thrown everything we had at them—fought them with our most advanced weapons as well as the full force of our psychic warriors. And still, the Tsakali had nearly destroyed us. Knowing that, could I really be mad at Hades for deceiving me to ensure our people's continued survival? I just wished he had trusted me with his true plan. That was the part that hurt the most.

At the sound of footsteps behind me, I opened my eyes but didn't turn around. My regulator was in its active amber state, suppressing my psychic senses. But I didn't need to be able to read minds to know who was behind me. There was only one person currently in the Alpha site who would have known to find me up here, in my old favorite haunt, let alone how to get up to the top of the tower in the first place. Hades.

His footsteps stopped a short way behind me. I figured he must have finished with Meg. I had checked on them in the Genetec tower—Hades' old domain—before coming up here. Hades finally had the necessary equipment up and running and was working his genetic magic on Meg, reversing her solar urticaria. She was already one hell of an asset to our team; once her deadly sun allergy was taken care of, she would be that much more valuable.

"From up here, it almost looks like nothing has changed," Hades said, his thoughts echoing mine from a moment ago.

I stretched my arms out along the railing and bowed my head. "Everything has changed."

Hades took a single step closer. "Everything?"

I thought back to the last time we were on this balcony together.

A hand curled around the back of my arm, and my eyes snapped open, training-turned-instinct driving my reaction. Not even five cycles of peace and inaction could tame the hard-earned instinct to fight from my body . . . even if this iteration of my body had never actually seen any real action.

With my free arm, I reached over my shoulder to draw my doru from the holster on my back, already anticipating the hum of energy that would radiate up my arm the instant my fingers made contact with the carved length of polished, golden orichalcum.

Fingers clasped onto my wrist, holding my hand in a steely grip. My fingertips stalled a hairsbreadth from the staff weapon.

"Why so on edge?" a man asked, the sound of his voice sending a not-unpleasant shiver cascading down my body. Hades.

He was the one person who should never, ever touch me. Because of our feelings for one another, it was reckless. Because of my position, it was beyond forbidden.

I narrowed my eyes, pressing my lips together. "You should know better," I said, ducking under my arm as I twisted around to face Hades. Standing so close to him, I had to raise my gaze to meet his icy blue eyes.

Hades looked as he always did—poised and polished, not a flaw on his pristine white suit, and not a hair out of place. Up this high, the ice dome's faint blue hue gave his blond hair a slightly silver tint.

My gaze lingered on his face for a moment, tracing the strong lines I'd yearned to touch for what felt like eons, before dropping to my wrist. To his long, graceful fingers. To the place where he was touching me.

My brain finally registered the danger. "What are you think-ing?" I hissed, shooting furtive glances to either side as I yanked my wrist free from his grasp.

Thankfully, the balcony was as empty as it had been when I'd first come up here. Well, almost as empty.

Anger boiled within me as my focus returned to Hades, to his hand hovering between us. I knew exactly what he'd been think-ing. That initial touch hadn't been a momentary lapse in judg-ment; it had been deliberate. He was trying to force my hand. Trying to make me decide before I was ready.

My eyes locked with his, the fond familiarity in his blue gaze unable to soothe my irritation.

Giving up everything, even for a lifetime on the surface with him—under the glorious sun—wasn't an easy choice. Excommu-nication was serious. It was a life sentence. And in time, a death sentence. If we abandoned the Alpha site, this cycle would be our last. The threat of mortality always hovered in the shadows, taunting my people. For us, it would become real.

Making the choice even harder, I still wasn't one hundred percent convinced that Hades' intentions were pure. No matter his earnest words over the years, I couldn't quite make myself believe that he, an ancient, Olympus-born man—a prince by birthright—would fall for someone like me.

Like most of the people living in the four remaining settle-ments here on Atlantis, I was a product of the technological advances made during the trip from Olympus to this idyllic planet. Genetic tinkering made me look more like the native anthropos than like a natural-born Olympian. I was hardly his equal—without my position as a revered Amazon warrior, Hades would never even know I existed.

His brow furrowed. "I thought we agreed to leave this—"

I sliced my head to the left, breaking our stare and focusing on some far-off point at the edge of the city where the grids of crops and green-turfed training fields met the ice wall.

"Peri?" There was hurt in Hades' voice. His hand inched closer to me, angling toward my arm.

I took a step back, one hand partially upraised. I couldn't look him in the eye, so I focused on his chin instead. The pale stubble covering his square jaw glistened in the filtered light. "I'm sorry, I—" I swallowed, my voice feeling too thick in my throat. "I just need more time."

"Time," Hades said bitterly. "That's the one thing we have too much of." He curled his upper lip in distaste. "And what do we do with it?" He took a step toward me, and I fought the urge to back up further. "Nothing. We do nothing. Because we're cowards."

My regulator was activated, the stone set into the silver disk hanging like a pendant from the chain around my neck glowing a steady, subtle amber, blocking my psychic abilities. Every once in a while, something still slipped through, but not often. And not now. But I didn't need to be able to read Hades' mind to pick out his true meaning. He'd said we were cowards, but he'd meant I was a coward.

I couldn't avoid his stare any longer. His words were a slap, knocking me out of the painful tangle of thoughts and emotions holding me captive. "I'm not a coward," I said, teeth gritted and glare hard. I was the best of the best, a highly skilled warrior equipped with the psychic gifts unique to my rank. I was an Amazon, damn it.

Hades leaned in, testing me. Would I back up? Lash out? Run? He was always testing me, it seemed. Maybe that was what made me doubt his feelings for me. Or maybe it was my fear.

He inched closer until I could feel the gentle caress of air brushing over my skin as he exhaled. He held my gaze, challenge clear in his eyes. "Prove it," he whispered.

· · ·

Emotions charged by the memory, I straightened and turned to face Hades. He stood close—closer than I had expected—and I automatically leaned back against the railing, my heart beating faster at his close proximity. My eyes locked with his, and my smile faded at the intensity of his ice-blue stare. At the hints of things unsaid. Undone. Unfulfilled. I licked my lips.

Hades raised a hand, brushing the backs of his fingers down my cheek.

I closed my eyes and leaned into the gentle caress. The emotions of the moment overwhelmed me, and I turned my face away to hide the tears leaking from between my eyelids. "Yes," I said, my voice little more than a whisper. "Everything."

Hades' hand fell away from my face.

I opened my eyes and sidestepped away, turning my back to him. Hastily, I wiped the tears from my cheeks.

"Peri . . ." The way he said my name, his voice raw and filled with longing, clawed at my heart. "I'm sorry."

I cleared my throat. "I think you should call me Cora," I told him. "It's less confusing that way."

Hades was quiet for a long moment. "I see," he finally said, like he had any right to be wounded by the harsh reality of our situation. Of *my* situation which *he* had caused.

Anger sparking, I spun around to face him, my stare hard and accusing. "Do you?" I said. "Do you really *see*? You know, I didn't ask to be like this—to be two people smashed together into one. To have my heart torn in two. This is your doing, Hades. I'm like this because of you." I jutted out my jaw, refusing to let my frustration wring more tears out of me. "You could have just let me go." My chin trembled, my fire fading as I realized part of me wished he had. "Why didn't you just let me go?"

Hades raised a hand, then let it drop. He swallowed several times, almost like he was choking on the words. "I couldn't," he finally managed to say. "I had nothing left. Nothing to look forward to. Nothing to keep me going. To let you go would have been to give up, and I—I just couldn't." He shook his head like he was locked in a silent argument with himself. "I couldn't do it."

I took a step toward him, my anger at this confusing situation boiling over. I hated feeling like anyone's happiness was tied to me, but there was no way to avoid the fact that both Raiden and Hades were looking to me for something I wasn't sure I would ever be able to give either of them. I loved them—both of them —and hurting them hurt me. But I didn't see any way to stop. It was so easy to blame Hades. To make him the focal point of my anger.

"You used me, Hades," I accused, ruthless and relentless in the verbal assault mounting in my mind. "I was a carrot on a stick. Some prize waiting for you at the end of your mission."

"No!" Hades gasped. He took a step toward me, reaching out for my arm, but I yanked it out of reach. "I loved you," he proclaimed, his eyes searching mine as he placed his open hand over his heart. "I *love* you still. I didn't know how everything would turn out. I didn't know you would be raised as a human, ignorant of your true self."

I thought back to the holodisk given to me by the Zari during my involuntary stay in the transformed Beta site. It was one of many, each created by Hades to address a different situation.

"Maybe you didn't know this would happen," I said, "but you knew it was a possibility. You knew I might end up like this, but you did it anyway. You set up your mazes and puzzles and claimed it was for the good of our people, but really it was for you. It was all for you—so you didn't have to live without your favorite pet."

Hades shook his head. "That's not—"

My hands balled into fists. "No more tricks, Hades," I snapped. "No more lies." Taking a deep breath, I raised one hand to deactivate my regulator. "Why don't you think this planet has a chance to survive the Tsakali? And why are the Tsakali hell-bent on destroying our people?"

Hades blinked, blindsided by the subject change. He eyed my regulator, the stone glowing a brilliant electric blue, and I sensed his mind shuffling through potential responses despite the effort I was putting into staying out of his head . . . for the moment.

"I want the truth," I told him. "The *whole* truth. In your logs, you referenced some prior history between the Tsakali and our people—before the war. You hinted that we helped them, that we gave them advanced technology. That we created them." I shook my head. "But that's not what I was taught. I was raised to believe the Tsakali are tech-hungry monsters. They have no conscience and no control. They conquer and consume and destroy." I narrowed my eyes. "But there's more to it, isn't there?"

I raised my eyebrows and set my jaw, crossing my arms over my chest, letting Hades see that I meant business. This was all or nothing. How he answered me now would determine what happened next—for us and for the mission.

Hades sighed, his neck bending under the weight of my questions. He combed his fingers through his loose hair and turned to the railing, staring out at the city. "The Tsakali were a gentle, nomadic race living on a dying planet," he began. "Their star was unstable, and their world was at risk." His fingers curled around the railing. "We transported them to a new world and set them up with the tech they would need to survive—a few chaos stones to power their new cities and some other things—and continued to trade with them for over a century." He bowed his head and closed his eyes, a single, bitter laugh shaking his chest. "We never thought they would become what they did."

Sensing the truth in his words, I moved closer, leaning my hip on the railing as I listened.

"Those gentle people changed," he went on, raising his head to stare out at the energy barrier. "That new place—their new situation—it changed them. We had opened their eyes to the universe, and they adapted, became hungry for more—more power, more tech, more time. Always *more*." He was quiet for a moment, battling his inner shame. "Seeking immortality, they developed advanced robotics tech and transferred their consciousnesses into synthetic host bodies. They were stronger and smarter than ever before. But when they moved into their new bodies, they lost something of themselves, some inner spark —what the people of this planet would call a soul."

I tilted my head to the side, eager for more.

"These new Tsakali frightened us," Hades admitted, "and when they came to us demanding we show them how to create chaos stones—and when we refused—they attacked. They infected our people with a nanotech biological weapon that rendered us infertile, claiming they could reverse the effect but would only do so after we shared the secret of how to create chaos stones. We refused."

He didn't need to go on. I could see the rest plainly in his mind. In that moment, he was an open book, inviting me to view his deepest, darkest secrets.

"And they declared war," I said, not as a question but as a statement of fact.

Hades nodded once. "If we wouldn't help them, we were no use to them, so they vowed to destroy us." Again, he was quiet for a moment. "And they've been hunting us ever since."

I didn't respond right away, giving both of us the time we needed to process what he had shared. Suddenly, a thought occurred to me—not bad, but potentially game-changing, at least, for the people of this planet. "So, if the Olympians aren't here when the Tsakali arrive," I said, "there's a chance the humans could resolve this peacefully, isn't there?"

Hades laughed bitterly. "Oh yes," he spat, "there's a very good chance. In fact, I could tell them exactly what they would need to do to survive—at least, for a time." He glanced at me, but only for a moment. "Tell the Tsakali how to create chaos stones."

In his mind, I could see what Hades' believed would happen next, and based on what I now knew, I had to agree it seemed like the most likely outcome. If the humans of Earth handed over the secret to creating chaos stones, the Tsakali would use their now abundant supply of chaos stones to reproduce endlessly. Like a cancer, they would spread across the universe, consuming and destroying everything in their path in their endless quest for *more*.

I gulped, horrified by that possibility. More than the people of this planet were at stake. "We can't let that happen," I said, sounding more confident than I felt.

"No," Hades agreed, "we can't." Finally, he looked at me with more than just a passing glance. "Peri—Cora," he corrected immediately. "I understand why you're angry with me. You should be. I deceived you, and I'm sorry, but you made your stance on evacuation clear, and I did what I believed was in the best interest of our people."

I groaned, my shoulders slumping and my head drooping. I wasn't angry with Hades. Not really. I was angry at the situation more than anything, and I was taking it out on Hades because he had made himself an easy target. But the situation was bigger than us and our complicated past. It was bigger even than the survival of our people. So, I had to be bigger, too.

I blew out a breath and straightened, pushing my shoulders back and holding my head high. My eyes locked with Hades' ice-blue stare. "I'm not mad at you," I told him, "and I understand why you lied. Maybe if you had explained your reasoning, I would have come around." I nodded my head to the side. "Or not." I laughed under my breath. "But now I agree, evacuation is our best option—maybe our only option."

My thoughts drifted back to my earlier tirade, and I felt the urge to explain why I had lashed out. "And I really am glad to be alive," I told him as I turned my attention to the city below, to the place where I have lived out the majority of my lifetimes, and carefully picked out the right words. "As Cora, I've been able to experience something I never had before." I shot Hades a sideways glance. "A family," I told him, flashing him a watery smile.

A crease formed between Hades' eyebrows as he listened quietly, attentively, his gaze skimming over the lines of my face.

"I have a mother who loves me more than anything else in the world," I continued, "and experiencing what that's like has shown me what a mockery Demeter made of the role." I scoffed, shaking my head as I recalled how highly I had revered the leader of the Order of Amazons—Mother, as we had been taught to call her—once upon a time. Before her betrayal had nearly doomed us all. "I have a home and people who I would do anything for and despite my sheltered upbringing, I've had a good life so far. I feel like Pinocchio, like I'm finally a real girl, which I know you won't understand because you've never heard of Pinocchio. I—I'm glad everything got screwed up and I was able to live this semi-normal life for a while. I'm just . . ."

Letting out a long, drawn-out sigh, I turned back to the railing, once again staring out at the city. "I'm adjusting. I'm confused. I'm still trying to figure out who I am when I'm Cora *and* Peri and what I want from life." My eyes stung with tears, but I didn't try to hide them this time. "I get that you spent literal millennia trying to bring me back, but you can't expect me to be ready or able to pick up where we left off before I died. I'm not the same person, and—and I need to get to know myself, and to get to know you and Raiden and everyone else. I just—" Tears crept over the brims of my eyelids and streaked down my cheeks. I bowed my head. "I wish people would stop expecting me to be someone I'm not so I can stop disappointing everyone."

Hades turned to me, reaching out to gently wipe a tear from

my cheek with the pad of his thumb. "You don't disappoint me, Cora," he said softly.

I looked at him. This was the first time he had called me "Cora" without stumbling over the name. It felt right, and some of the tension within me eased.

"You surprise me," he said, the corner of his mouth rising with a secretive smile. The way he was gazing at me sent a tingle of anticipation zinging through me. "Truth be told," Hades confessed, "I'm quite enjoying it."

A breathy laugh escaped from my lips. In that moment, I wanted him to lean in, to kiss me. Regardless of what I had told him, I craved the rush elicited by his forbidden touch. But I could see in his mind that he was committed to respecting my wishes, to giving me the time I needed to figure myself out. If I wanted something to happen between us, I would have to make the first move, and I wasn't ready to take that leap. A willingness to *be* kissed and a willingness to kiss were two entirely different things.

I activated my regulator, wanting to give Hades his privacy, and turned to face him. Reaching out, I captured his hand, noting how different it was from Raiden's. How could these two men who I loved so deeply be so different? They were day and night, rough and smooth, human and *other*. But I loved them, both of them, with all my heart.

Acting on impulse, I leaned in toward Hades and rose to my toes to gently press my lips to his cheek. He became statue-still, as though he was afraid the movement would shatter the moment. I dropped my heels back down and studied his haunting beauty, reading his emotions the old-fashioned way.

"Thank you," I whispered.

Hades' expression turned quizzical, but I didn't elaborate. I couldn't. Not right now. I offered him a tight-lipped smile, then turned and walked away.

[15]

I sat on my knees beside Meg's bedroll on the floor of the gephyra chamber. Meg lay stretched out on her back in the sleeping bag, her eyes closed, recovering from the hours upon hours of gene therapy. She was weak, her skin waxen and sweaty, and violent shivers wracked her body every now and again. Though she appeared to be asleep, I sensed her awareness through our bond, muddled by the shooting pains wreaking havoc on her nerve endings and cramping her muscles.

I dabbed a cool, damp cloth against Meg's forehead, then wiped down her cheeks and neck, providing what little comfort I could. I hated seeing her in so much pain.

"It will be worth it"—she sucked in a shaky breath—"in the end." She swallowed roughly, then coughed as the saliva caught in her throat. Her pain levels spiked at the sharp movement. "I just wish—"

"Shhh . . ." I rested the damp cloth across her forehead and grabbed her nearest hand, squeezing it gently. Talking was only increasing her pain, and there was no need between us, not when I could sense every turn of her mind, just as she could mine.

I knew Meg wished, desperately, that she could come with us

as we journeyed through the gephyra to explore the lost colonies. Not only did she want to see the distant worlds for herself, but she wanted to protect me. She had pledged her life to mine in the sweltering rainforest, the day we had linked our regulators and formed our bond, and she had meant it.

"You'll be with me the whole time," I told her. I tapped my temple with a fingertip. "You'll be right up here, seeing everything I see. Next best thing to actually being there." Or, at least, I hoped that would be the case. The only way to know for sure if our bond could span the lightyears between worlds was to travel across a gephyra bridge and find out.

Meg attempted to smile, but a tremor struck her body just then, and she groaned, her teeth clenched, and her eyes squeezed shut.

The way I understood it, Hades had essentially re-written her genetic code, and the cells throughout her body were being replaced at an unnatural rate. Once the cellular transformation was complete, she would be better than ever. Meg 2.0, the baddest of the baddasses. But until then, she was as weak and helpless as a sick baby, and it broke my heart to see her like this.

I curled my other hand around hers, giving her all the support I could while she suffered through the fit, until her body relaxed once more. "Don't worry about me," I told her, rubbing the back of her hand with my thumb. "Just worry about getting better, and the next time I travel off-world, I promise you'll be coming along."

Meg's eyes fluttered open, and a weak smile touched her lips.

"Get some rest," I said as I placed her hand on her middle and sat back on my heels. Hands on the floor, I stood and retrieved my doru from where I had leaned it against the wall, then joined the others huddled around the gephyra's freestanding control panel nearby.

Our packs were lined up in front of the control panel, and Hades stood on the opposite side with Emi, explaining to her how to operate the gephyra controls as he entered the coordinates of our first destination. Raiden, Fiona, and my mom stood off to either side of the control panel, watching the lesson. Both Fiona and my mom wore hoplon suits, which would provide them plenty of protection, even without being reinforced by a latent infusion of psychic energy. Since hoplon suits had only ever been made for female Olympians—as the sole bearers of the psychic gifts—Raiden and Hades had settled with wearing Gargarean armor. The bulkier suits that had been worn by the mundane, male Olympian warriors were still an upgrade from any human-made protective gear, but they were no hoplon suits.

The overall mood was somber, with an undercurrent of excitement about the coming interplanetary trip. Hades and I had explained the true mission—to find an Olympian ark ship and use it to evacuate the remains of the Olympians along with as many humans as possible—as well as the reason why. Coming to grips with the fact that, barring some miracle, Earth was beyond saving, wasn't easy for any of them. I still struggled with denial, my mind constantly working to find another solution, and I was surprised by how quickly the others had jumped on board with the plan. None had accepted that Earth couldn't be saved, but they understood why the evacuation had to be done. At least this way, some humans would be guaranteed survival.

My mom held out an arm as I approached, and I let her pull me into a side hug, her arm curling around my waist. "How's Meg doing?" she asked.

I draped my arm around my mom's shoulders. "She's in a lot of pain, but she'll get better." I sighed. "I just wish I didn't have to leave her like this."

My mom gave my waist a squeeze. "Emi will take good care of her," she said, and I knew she was right.

Emi would be staying behind with Meg while the rest of us ventured through the gephyra to the lost colonies—worlds colonized by my people long ago. Each colony had failed for its own reason. The last contact my people had had with any of the lost colonies had been over twelve thousand years ago when that ill-fated team of Amazon warriors had traveled off-world to search for a chaos stone. I would forever feel guilty for damning my spearsisters to such a brutal banishment. After all, they had only been following orders. But Hades and I had done what needed to be done, sacrificing a handful of lives to save an entire planet. Just as we would do again, sacrificing the planet to save the universe, because the Tsakali *had* to be stopped.

"Remember," Hades told Emi, "the bridge between worlds must be active for the communication system to work, should you need to reach us for any reason."

We all wore Olympian communication patches behind our ears since we weren't sure if our two-way radios would work across the bridge created between gephyras.

Hades slid my mom's journal across the smooth surface of the control panel, leaving it directly in front of Emi. "We'll leave the bridge active," he continued, "but there is always a chance for disruption. We will not always be within sight of the gephyra on our end, so we may not know if the bridge has closed. I saved the coordinates of our destination as the default setting, should you need to reestablish the bridge yourself, and recorded the coordinates of each of the colonies we will be visiting in Diana's book." He tapped the leather cover of the journal.

"I understand," Emi said with a nod, picking up the journal and hugging it to her chest. Her eyes skipped over to Raiden, just for a moment, and with my regulator activated, I could only imagine the fear she felt at thinking about her son—her only child—being on an entirely different planet from her. If the bridge collapsed, the coordinates within the journal were the only tether connecting her to Raiden.

"I will contact you before collapsing the active bridge when we are ready to travel to a new planet to alert you to the coordi-nates of our next destination and to remotely reset the home system's default setting," Hades explained to Emi. "Once we arrive at our new destination, I will establish a bridge between the new gephyra and this one." He pointed to the dormant gephyra behind me with his chin.

Again, Emi nodded.

Hades pressed a small, golden button on the control panel. "This button initiates the activation sequence. Unless overridden, it will establish a bridge between this gephyra and the one at the default coordinates."

A quiet humming started behind me, the volume amplifying by the second. I turned around to face the gephyra in time to see half of the innermost ring, about ten inches thick and eight feet in diameter, rising from the center of the golden platform as the other half sank into the portion of the machine buried in the floor. Ancient, Olympian glyphs representing the coordinates of our destination glowed silver on the ring's surface, brightening as the ring spun.

The others were staring now, and I didn't need to deactivate my regulator to sense their curiosity and awe. None of them had known what to expect, but this clearly wasn't it.

That lone ring made a slow rotation around an invisible axis, eventually ending up flush with the rest of the platform once more. When the innermost ring rose again, a second joined it, just outside the first, spinning on an opposing axis. Just like with the first ring, glyphs glowed along its surface. The brief moment that both rings sat flush with the rest of the platform, a third ring joined them, fitting perfectly around the second, and yet again spinning on its own unique and invisible axis.

The process continued until a seventh ring joined the inner six, at least fourteen feet in diameter. All seven rings glowed with those ancient silver glyphs. The rotation of the rings picked up speed until they were moving too quickly for the naked eye to track. They seemed to disappear, giving way to a seven-foot-tall quicksilver orb standing in the dead center of the platform.

"That is . . .," Raiden started but trailed off with a slow shake of his head.

"Wow," my mom said, her voice hushed.

"Yeah," Raiden agreed. "It's very *wow*."

I exchanged a look with Hades over my shoulder, then glanced at Raiden and my mom sidelong, finally landing on Fiona, who gawked at the opening to a bridge that spanned worlds. A sly grin spread across my lips. "Now, are you impressed?"

Fiona guffawed, not tearing her eyes from the huge quick-silver orb. "Uh, yeah."

My mom rubbed her hands together, her eyes filled with the hunger of a seasoned explorer catching her first glimpse of an as yet unexplored frontier.

"The bridge is now fully formed," Hades informed us. A moment later, he sent a baseball-sized drone across the bridge and pulled up the screen on the holoband wrapped around his forearm as he assessed the readings being fed back to him. With a nod, he collapsed the holographic screen and lowered his arm. "It is safe on the other side," he said. "We may depart when ready."

Taking a deep breath, I turned my back to the gephyra and propped my doru against the backside of the control panel. "No time like the present," I said as I reached for my pack. I settled the loaded bag on my shoulders, then reclaimed my weapon.

As the others donned their packs and readied for the journey, I deactivated my regulator, closing my eyes for a moment as I focused on blocking out the thoughts and emotions of everyone around me. We were heading into the relative unknown, and I needed to be on high alert. Their minds would only serve to distract me.

Once my mental blocks were in place and my mind was rela-tively clear, I opened my eyes, pleased to find the others with their packs snug on their backs and ready to go.

"Do you have any final questions?" Hades asked Emi as he made a small adjustment to his right shoulder strap.

Emi shook her head. "I don't think so."

Hades nodded once to her, then turned to me and raised his eyebrows. "Are we ready?"

I inhaled deeply, my blood humming with excitement at the coming adventure and my heart filled with hope that we still might find a way to save Earth.

Raiden moved closer to Hades until they were standing side by side. "Good to go?"

I looked at the two men who occupied different parts of my heart, guilt twisting in my gut. I didn't want to choose between them. I wanted them both. The Peri part of me saw no problem with such an arrangement, but the Cora part of me believed such a thing would be impossible.

Regardless of what might happen between the three of us in the future, I refused to play games with their hearts, or with mine. I would not make this situation any more difficult than it already was. Once I had a solid grasp on who I was, now, and who I wanted to be in the future, I vowed I would revisit this tangled situation.

Or, we might all die on some distant planet, in which case, it wouldn't matter.

Spirits oddly lifted by that thought, I turned my back to the men I loved and marched toward the gephyra. Even with their thoughts and emotions blocked from my mind, I sensed the others following behind me—first Raiden and Hades, then my mom and Fiona.

I paused at the base of the gephyra, giving us all a moment to grow accustomed to the uncomfortable static sensation emitted by the open bridge. I gripped my doru with both hands, charging the focus crystal until it blazed electric blue, ascended the steps, and plunged into the unknown.

[16]

Doru at the ready, I stepped out of the enormous quicksilver orb
that marked the far side of the gephyra bridge and jogged down
the trio of steps to the base of the platform, where I stopped to
scan my surroundings. I shrugged off the disorientation and
physical discomfort that came hand-in-hand with gephyra travel
as I looked around. And then I frowned. There was no sense of
Meg or our bond in my mind.

The gephyra was the only thing I could see that appeared to
be undamaged amidst a sea of ruins in a barren landscape. This
was nothing like the relatively intact Olympian settlements back
on Earth. I glanced at the gephyra, comparing it to the wasted
ruins surrounding me.

Not much could even put a scratch in pure orichalcum, so it
wasn't surprising that the gephyra looked to be in good shape,
but most Olympian structures were built using various
orichalcum alloys that strengthened them if not making them
quite so indestructible. Apparently, the orichalcum alloy used
during the construction of this settlement hadn't been strong
enough to withstand whatever had happened here.

Hades emerged from the gephyra and trotted down the stairs

to join me, his eyes scanning the wasteland. A crease formed between his brows, the only outward sign that he was troubled by finding the colony in such a state.

Raiden came next, stumbling down the steps and dropping to one knee as soon as he reached the dusty ground. He bowed his head, taking deep, gasping breaths. Fiona followed, running down the steps and bending over to hurl up the contents of her stomach. My mom came through last and crouched with her hands on her knees, breathing hard as she looked around.

I moved closer to Fiona and rubbed her back as her stomach convulsed for a third time. "You guys all right?" I asked, looking from my mom to Raiden.

"Traveling through the gephyra can take some getting used to," Hades said, mild amusement curving his lips, though it didn't chase the shadows from his eyes.

"A little warning would have been nice," Raiden said, his voice rough, but his breathing had slowed. He rose to his feet and placed his hands on his hips as he looked around.

"Sorry," I said, flashing him an apologetic smile. With everything going on, the idea of warning them hadn't even crossed my mind.

Raiden's eyes narrowed as he continued his slow scan of the ruins surrounding us. "What the hell happened here? It looks like someone dropped a nuke on this place."

My mom caught my eye, then glanced down at herself. "Do these fancy suits protect us from radiation?"

"For the most part, yes," I told her. If her hoplon suit had been flush with psychic energy, she wouldn't have had much to worry about. I could activate the energy helmet function, which would lock me in a self-contained, safe environment. But for my mom and Fiona—not to mention the guys in their Gargarian gear —that wasn't an option. "But your head is exposed," I added, "and the suit won't protect you from breathing in particles in the air, so . . ." I looked to Hades, who was studying the small holographic screen projected up from his holoband, double-checking the readings from the drone hovering nearby. "Do we need masks?" I asked.

Hades shook his head. "The levels of harmful radiation are well within the realm of normal." He lowered his arm, his focus hitching on me before sliding over to my mom. "We're safe," he assured her. "Whatever happened here, happened a long time ago."

"Did everyone make it through safely?" Emi asked, the comms patch conducting her voice through the bones of my skull into my ear.

"Yep," my mom said. "We're all present and accounted for." She glanced at Fiona, who was still doubled over, though the heaving seemed to have stopped. Now, she repeatedly spat saliva onto the barren ground, no doubt attempting to clear her mouth of the taste of bile. "You didn't happen to pack any Dramamine into our first aid kits, did you, Em?" my mom asked.

"No," Emi said, "but I have some here. Do you want me to send it through?"

Fiona waved a hand at my mom and shook her head. "No," she said, her voice raspy. "It'll only make me sleepy." She straightened, wiping her mouth with the back of her hand. "I'll be fine. I just need a minute." When I patted her back, she flashed me a queasy smile. "Thanks."

I returned her smile. "You good?" I asked, raising my eyebrows.

Fiona nodded. She still looked a little green around the gills, but I could sense that the nausea was waning.

I turned away from her, placing my hands on my hips as I surveyed the lackluster landscape. "I'm a little surprised the gephyra here works," I said, glancing at Hades. A gephyra was powered by chaos energy, either indirectly from the chaos stone powering a city or ship or directly through less potent chaos fragments stored in the guts of the gephyra itself. But I wouldn't have expected either to be present in a settlement that had been so devastated.

Hades' eyes met mine, just for a moment. "The chaos fragments are still in place." He must have run a scan for traces of chaos energy.

"Huh," I said, chewing on the inside of my cheek. "Alright, well, let's split up and spread out," I told the others. "See if any parts of this place are in better shape." I looked at my mom. "Mom, you go with Hades." I glanced over my shoulder. "Fio, stick close to Raiden . . . just in case. Anything made of orichalcum should have survived—like the gephyra. If you find anything that appears to be in good shape, let Hades know."

My attention returned to the ruins. A few taller structures rose above the rest, the remains of once soaring towers. "I'll get to higher ground to see if the destruction is localized to this area. Could be we'll find a better location to search."

Hades locked eyes with Raiden. "Don't venture too far from the gephyra. I don't expect we'll be here long."

Frowning, I headed into the ruins, picking my way over rubble and rusted shards of metal. What a depressing way to start our quest. Hades' search for energy signatures would have tapped into the satellite system our people set up around every planet we colonized. The fact that he hadn't found anything didn't bode well for our search for a functioning ark ship.

I sensed the others branching out in pairs, my mom with Hades, and Fiona with Raiden.

"What do you think happened here?" Fiona asked over the comms patch. "Was it the Tsakali?"

I picked my way through the ruins, heading for the tallest remains of a tower within my line of sight, still some sixty yards out. It reached up thirty or forty feet toward the murky sky, ravaged edges like rusted claws.

"Might have been," came Hades' response. "We, too, have weapons capable of such destruction. Every colony is equipped with the means to self-destruct. There's no way to determine if this was self-inflicted."

"You think they might've done this to themselves?" Fiona asked. "But why would they do that?"

The conversation over the comms went momentarily silent. When Hades finally responded, his voice was somber, and his words sent shivers trickling down my spine. "For the greater good," he said.

We all knew what he meant. If the Tsakali had found this colony, then it would have been better for Olympian-kind—for the whole universe—if this place and all the knowledge it contained was destroyed rather than let the Tsakali get their hands on the secret of how to create chaos stones.

When I finally reached the crumbling tower, I pressed my hand to one unsteady post, reinforcing it with psychic energy. My hoplon suit might protect me from being crushed or impaled should the decrepit remains of the building collapse as I was climbing, but it would take the others time to dig me out, and we were racing against the clock. Hades had predicted the Tsakali ships would arrive in two months, and we needed to find an ark ship, load the Olympian consciousness orbs and preserved embryos onto the ship, self-destruct all Olympian sites on the planet, somehow convince the humans to destroy all knowledge of how to create a chaos stone, load up as many humans as possible, and get the hell out of there while we still had time to outrun the Tsakali. So, yeah, we didn't have any time to spare.

Once I was certain the structure would hold, I sheathed my doru on my back and started to climb. The view from the top was no less disappointing than from the ground. The destruction spread out as far as I could see.

"It's a wasteland, guys," I shared remotely. "I think we should call it and move on to another colony. We're just wasting time here."

I quickly climbed down and hurried back to the gephyra. I

was the last to arrive, having ventured out the farthest, but I easily settled into the sober mood.

Bunched together near the gephyra platform, we waited while Hades remotely reprogramed the gephyra back on Earth with the coordinates of our next destination. Once he was finished, he disconnected the bridge, waited for the rings to settle back into the platform, then opened the manual control panel in the base of the gephyra platform and input the new coordinates.

The rings started to spin, and as soon as the quicksilver orb appeared, water gushed out through the bridge opening.

"Shit!" I shouted, backing up a few steps to keep from having my feet washed out from under me by the current. The others scrambled farther away.

Hades clung to the base of the platform, his head bowed to avoid drowning under the deluge.

I raised my hands and created an electric-blue energy barrier snug around the bridge opening, containing the outpouring of water. "Shut it down!" Clearly, the gephyra on the far side of the bridge was submerged under water. For all intents and purposes, that colony truly was lost.

Hades coughed and sputtered, catching his breath. Moments later, the quicksilver orb vanished, and the rings slowed, once again settling into the platform. I released the energy barrier, and water splashed down around the gephyra, soaking Hades one more time.

Hades scrubbed his hands over his face, wiping away the remaining water, then reached into the control panel. He entered the next set of coordinates. The rings started to spin, and I held my breath as the quicksilver orb formed.

When nothing unexpected happened, I let out the held breath and drew my doru. Hades sent the scouting drone across the bridge first, and I watched him stare at the screen of his holoband, waiting for his nod telling me that the environment on the new planet was safe.

Hades' eyes scanned the readings, then shifted to me, and he nodded.

I charged the doru's focus crystal with psychic energy, gripped the staff in both hands, and marched across the bridge to another planet.

[17]

I emerged from the bridge and was smacked in the face with a wall of dry heat and blinding sunlight as sand ground beneath my boots. The gephyra was on a raised dais, a dozen or so weathered granite steps rising from the top of a tower, and the arid desert had swallowed much of the settlement surrounding the tower.

I jogged down the steps, stopping when I reached the thick layer of bone-dry sand gathered on the walkway surrounding the platform and surveyed the half-buried settlement spreading out around the tower. It was clear that this city had been designed using the standard settlement layout, like the Alpha site with land rings separating by canals, and it looked to be in decent shape, especially compared to the first colony we had visited. The exposed glass and metal of the towers should have gleamed in the sunlight, but the sand had worn down their exteriors over however many thousands of years this colony had been abandoned.

"Looks alright," I told the others through the comms patch. "Come on through."

They emerged from the gephyra in the same order as before, Hades first, followed by Raiden, then Fiona, and then my mom. The trip didn't seem quite so upsetting to the novice travelers this time, though Fiona did have to sit down on one of the higher steps and put her head between her knees.

Hades immediately disconnected the bridge, then reconnected with Earth.

After we had checked in with Emi, my mom trudged through the sand toward the place where Hades and I stood together at the railing surrounding the top of the tower, studying the much more promising remains of what had once been a sprawling and glorious Olympian city. "Why are these colonies all above ground when the settlements on Earth were hidden?" she asked.

"An astute observation," Hades said as he squinted, staring off in the distance, and nodded slowly. "When we left Olympus," he explained, "only the *Tartarus* and one other ship, the *Elysium*, were tasked with settling on an inhabited planet with the purpose of hybridizing the native olympianoid life-forms with our species. The others set out to settle uninhabited planets with the hopes that they could remain hidden from the Tsakali until they found a way to dispel the nano-virus plaguing our people. The hope was that the cure would be discovered before cloning sickness rendered our DNA nonviable."

I turned to my mom, continuing the explanation. "Some of the colonies fell before we lost contact, but after a virus virtually wiped out the Beta site on Earth, Poseidon grew too paranoid to allow any off-world contact and ordered the colonies off-limits. We still checked in with them every once in a while—long-range communications only—but one by one they stopped responding until none responded any longer and all were considered lost."

Raiden joined us. "No pressure or anything . . ."

I laughed under my breath and muttered, "No kidding." There was a good chance that Hades and I weren't only the last living Olympians on Earth, but the last living Olympians *at all*. That kind of pressure would crush us if we let it.

I pointed to a tower jutting out of the sand nearby. Assuming this settlement followed the standard layout to a T, that particular building would have belonged to Genetec and hosted all the city's genetic research and cloning. "Hades, take Raiden and check out Genetec. See if there's anything useful there." If the settlers here had made any progress in counteracting the nano-virus, that invaluable data would be stored there.

I glanced at my mom. "Mom, you and Fio come with me."

Raiden looked uncomfortable with being paired up with Hades, but Hades didn't seem the least bit bothered by it.

Hades caught my eye. "I assume you're heading down to the mainframe?"

I nodded. Assuming this settlement's power core was still in place—and still functioning—I could run a search of the settle-ment's inventory from down there and find out definitively if there was an ark ship here. Plus, it wouldn't hurt to get our hands on another power core.

Hades and Raiden headed for the door that would lead them into the central tower, where they could descend to sand level before crossing over to the Genetec building.

I turned and climbed back up the steps to check on Fiona, who was still sitting on a stair at the base of the gephyra. "How are you doing?"

"Bleh . . ." She raised her head, laughing miserably. "Motion sickness is the worst. All I did was walk through a big silver blob to another planet. I didn't even get in a flying freaking saucer. I just"—she walked her fingers over her knee—"*walked*."

I patted her shoulder. "It should get easier," I said, crossing my index and middle fingers, just for a second.

Fiona blew out a breath. "Something to look forward to . . ."

I flashed her a conciliatory smile and held out my hand to help her to her feet. Once she was up and seemed stable, I started toward the door Hades and Raiden had used. The interior of the building was nearly identical to the central tower in the Alpha site, down to the endless administrative floors and the staircase spiraling around the glass-encased lift at the heart of the building. When we approached the lift, the door slid open, and I grinned. If the lift worked, the city had power—either a functioning power core or an actual chaos stone. The latter, I doubted, considering Hades had likely already scanned for all traces of chaos energy. But a power core was still a great prize.

We rode the lift down to the sublevel and made our way into the mainframe chamber. I held my breath as we approached the column in the center of the space, a part of me still hoping to find another chaos stone. I slid the panel in the column open and exhaled my disappointment. No chaos stone. Just a power core.

Hands on my hips, I stared at the humming power core and chewed on the inside of my cheek. Any chaos stone that may have been here was long gone, probably stolen by the Tsakali or used to power a ship carrying the people fleeing from this planet.

Eyes narrowed, I scanned the area around us, then turned to face my mom and Fiona. "Look around, check every nook and cranny—there might be a containment box hidden down here, like the one we used to hold the chaos stone back on Earth."

While they searched, I activated the master control console nearby. A large holoscreen popped up above the console, and I raised a hand to swipe across the floating screen to move through several menus and submenus until I reached the inventory section. I narrowed it down to the transportation sector and scrolled through the types of ships assigned to this planet. The name of this colony's ark ship, the *Asphodel*, was grayed out, indicating that it was currently off-world. Disappointing, but not necessarily surprising. I checked the logs to find out how long ago the ship had left, and why—purely for curiosity's sake. That knowledge wouldn't help us with our current predicament, but it would tell me more about why the settlers had abandoned this colony.

According to the logs, the Asphodel had departed nearly fifteen thousand Olympian years ago, translating to a little over twelve thousand Earth years. It matched up with the timeline of when we lost contact with the other colonies. Apparently, the settlers here had left after detecting Tsakali scouts within their star system. A note from the colony's Imperial scion, Aphrodite, to any Olympians who ventured here after their departure let me know that volunteers had remained behind to destroy all information and tech relating to the creation of chaos stones.

I glanced at the humming power core tucked away in its little recess in the column nearby. It was in good shape, unlike the power core in the Alpha site back on Earth. I supposed that was due to the arid conditions here.

With a sigh, I shut down the holoscreen and headed back over to the column. I placed a hand on my hip and stared at the power core. "I ran a search. No ship, but the power core is in decent shape," I said over the comms patch. "Hades, how about you?"

"I've taken the storage drive containing all of their research and a few replacement parts for the Omega site," Hades informed me, "but a few things are missing."

"Probably taken on the ark ship when they fled," I grumbled.

"Ah. Yes, that is likely," he said. "A preliminary scan of their research suggests they made some headway with preventing cloning disease, though they made no discernable headway regarding the nano-virus."

I tilted my head to the side, considering the new information. "That's better than nothing, I suppose."

"Indeed, it is," he agreed. "We're heading back to the gephyra now."

"Sounds good," I said, eyeing the power core. "Do you want the power core?"

"If it's not too much trouble . . ."

I groaned inwardly, thinking about climbing all those stairs to the top of the tower carrying the power core. Those things weren't light. "No trouble at all," I told him, sheathing my doru and reaching into the column. I gripped either side of the power core and said, "Removing the power core now." With a grunt, I yanked the core free and lifted it out of the column. "Sorry guys, looks like we'll all be taking the stairs back up."

Fiona groaned through the comms patch, and the sound became audible to my ears as she trudged back into view. "You couldn't have let us ride the lift up first?"

I snorted and shook my head, tucking the power core under my arm like a lead football. "Misery loves company," I told her, then led the way back to the lift—and the stairway that spiraled around it.

My mom, Fiona, and I traded off carrying the power core up the first fifteen floors, at which point Hades and Raiden caught up to us. The guys took their turns, but eventually, the power core ended up back in my arms. I was carrying it when we emerged onto the roof of the central tower and quickly delivered it through the gephyra to Earth.

As soon as I returned, Hades shut down the active bridge and input the coordinates to our next destination. The gephyra hummed, the rings spun, and the quicksilver orb that marked the opening of a new bridge formed. But it winked out before Hades could even guide the scouting drone across the gleaming barrier.

I looked at him, my eyes narrowing. "What the hell was that?"

"I'm not sure," Hades said before ducking his head back into the bowels of the gephyra. He established the bridge again, but the same thing happened almost immediately.

I moved closer to him, crouching down to peer into the sheltered recess housing the gephyra's manual controls. "What's the problem?"

Hades fiddled with the controls. "I'm not sure," he repeated. "The connection is unstable for some reason."

I straightened and planted my hands on my hips, my stare fixing on the gephyra's rings as they resettled in the platform. "What could cause an unstable connection?"

Hades stilled for a moment and glanced at me over his shoulder. "Celestial drift, if unaccounted for, but the system's internal programming should self-correct the moment the bridge is established." He returned to adjusting the gephyra's complex settings. "It's almost like we're tripping an auto disconnect sequence set up on the other side," he went on, his voice slightly muffled.

I frowned, my spidey sense tingling. "Should we move on to the next colony?"

"I can manually override the other gephyra's ability to control the bridge," Hades said. "I just need to . . . there. Done." He emerged from the gephyra's underbelly and remained on his knees as the golden rings started to spin.

When the quicksilver orb appeared, I counted to ten, not expecting to make it past seven. When I hit twenty and the bridge was still active, I looked at Hades sidelong. "Is it safe to cross?"

Hades rose to his feet and used his holoband to guide the scouting drone across the bridge. Once the drone vanished, Hades fixed his gaze on me, a faint smirk twisting his lips. "Is traveling through the gephyra ever completely safe?"

I held his stare for a long moment. "Well, how does it look?" I asked, pointing to the quicksilver orb with my chin.

Hades checked the readings on the screen of his holoband. "It's dark—no visual, all the environmental readings fall within the range of acceptable."

I climbed the first step, then the second, and drew my doru. I paused to look back at the others. "Wait for my signal," I reminded them, and then I stepped onto the bridge.

The world was engulfed in darkness, with periodic flashes of light, and it felt like I was falling. Drowning. Being torn apart. But then I was through to the other side. I jogged down the steps and froze.

A shimmering yellow energy barrier enclosed the platform, encircled by a dozen Amazon warriors, their dorus charged, the focus crystals aimed at me.

[18]

I was an ice sculpture, frozen by the stares of my spearsisters. Other Amazon warriors. Part of me—most of me—had believed I would never see another Amazon again. Not in the flesh, at least.

Grappling with shock, my mind slogged through a series of semi-related thoughts. I wasn't the last of my kind. Hades and I weren't the last Olympians. We could ask these Amazons for help. Why weren't they lowering their dorus? Couldn't they see that I wasn't their enemy? That I was one of them?

Slowly, cautiously, I crouched down, setting my doru on the smooth, polished floor. It was some kind of marble, from the looks of it. Just as slowly, I straightened, raising my empty hands in surrender.

I scanned the sharp, angled Olympian features of the Amazons, searching for familiar faces. I found none.

"Hades," I said, keeping my voice low as I spoke to him through the comms patch. "Cross over. The rest of you, stay put."

"On my way," Hades said, not hesitating for a moment.

Raiden's voice came immediately after Hades finished speaking. "What is it, Cora?"

Hades emerged from the gephyra, his presence a comfort in this crazy situation. I felt his mind draw closer as he descended the steps.

"Olympians," I told the others. "And not necessarily friendly ones."

Hades stopped beside me, and in my peripheral vision, I watched him raise his hands over his head, mimicking my pose of surrender. "Have they said anything?" he asked me, his voice hushed.

I shook my head the barest amount.

Without warning, the golden energy barrier vanished, and one of the Amazon warriors surrounding us stepped forward, her doru still trained on me. Her mind was blocked by an impenetrable psychic wall. There was something familiar about her features, though I didn't recognize her. With her dark hair and hawkish stare, she reminded me a bit of Demeter, which was more than a little unsettling.

The Amazon's steps faltered as her focus shifted from me to Hades, and her eyes widened dramatically. "Hades?"

"Artemis!" Hades exclaimed.

My mouth fell open.

I knew of Artemis, if only by reputation. She was Hades' younger sister and a renowned warrior. Demeter had held the highest rank of Mother among the Order of Amazons on Earth, but Artemis had been the true Amazon leader back on Olympus. She had left years before the Tsakali attacked to establish a secondary homeworld for our people. Hers was the first colony ever settled by Olympians, but it had been lost shortly after the war began. Destroyed by the Tsakali, or so we had thought.

I dropped to one knee and bowed my head, watching her in my peripheral vision.

Hades took a step forward but stopped when Artemis shifted

her aim from me to him. "Don't move," she ordered. "I can't let you get too close to me. The risk of infection is too great."

At first, I thought she meant that she and her people were infected by something contagious. But Hades connected the dots faster than I did, realizing the opposite was true.

"You are not infected by the nano-virus?" He said, equal parts statement and question.

My head snapped up, and I gaped at Artemis. It wasn't possible. *All* Olympians were infected by the nano-virus. Period.

Artemis shook her head. "No, we're not," she said gravely. "And we'd like to keep it that way."

"The Olympians of this world can truly still reproduce naturally?" Hades clarified.

Artemis confirmed with a nod.

"But how?" Bafflement wafted off Hades in waves. "After so long . . ." Hades shook his head. "The Tsakali infected all Olympian worlds. How is this possible?"

Artemis narrowed her eyes. "How long, exactly?"

"Sixteen millennia," Hades told her, speaking in Olympian years. "But surely you would know that, unless . . ." He tilted his head to the side, studying her. "Why is it you are still alive if your people can reproduce naturally? You would have no need of cloning."

The corner of Artemis's mouth lifted in the faintest of smiles. "Ah, but I think you already know the answer to your own question, brother."

Hades nodded to himself, and I could feel his astonishment. "You erected a time dilation field around this planet," he said, his voice filled with awe. "You knew you couldn't hide from the Tsakali, so instead, you slowed time, hoping the rest of us would find a way to defeat them while you hid away in your little bubble." There was a sharp edge to his final words, and I felt anger simmering within him, growing stronger the more he thought through the implications of his theory.

I looked up at him, finding a sneer curling his lips.

"I never knew you to be a coward, little sister," Hades said, his stare hardening to a glare.

"It's not cowardice to know when to fight, and when to run," Artemis snapped.

Tension mounted, causing a rapid unraveling of the situation. If I didn't grab onto a string of sanity now, I feared there might not be any left to salvage what was left of this miraculous encounter.

I cleared my throat and stood, drawing the attention of the Amazon warriors encircling us back to me. "It's an honor to meet you, Mother," I said, offering Artemis a deep bow. When I straightened, her hawkish stare was fixed on me.

"Aren't you quite the curiosity," she said, scrutinizing me from head to toe. "An Amazon, but not an Olympian."

I flushed, equal parts offended and ashamed. I couldn't help the way I looked, but it was clear from the way Artemis was studying me that she found me somehow deficient.

"She is as Olympian as you or me," Hades said, coming to my defense.

Artemis glanced at Hades, but her focus quickly returned to me. "Is she now?" She cocked her head to the side.

I fought the urge to squirm under her scrutiny.

"Engineered?" Artemis asked.

"We altered the appearance of the workers created on board the *Tartarus* to blend in better with the people of our destination planet," Hades explained.

Artemis raised her eyebrows. "And raised one to full-powered Amazon. I had no idea our dear sister was so progressive."

I gritted my teeth, quickly tiring of being discussed like I wasn't even there. Or worse, like I wasn't a person. Like I was a thing.

Hades cleared his throat. "Someone may have planted a seed of the idea in her mind . . ."

I looked at him, stunned by the revelation. But now was not the time to be distracted by the past, and I tucked the matter away in my mind for later and returned my attention to Artemis. "We've come here because the Tsakali are on their way to our world—to Atlantis," I said, using the Olympian name for Earth. "Our only hope to save our people is to find an ark ship to evacuate those who remain before the Tsakali arrive." I left out the part where *those who remain* weren't actually currently living.

Artemis stared at me for a long moment, then looked at Hades. "Will you issue a self-destruct on the world?"

Hades was quiet for a long moment, but I could feel his commitment to protecting the universe, so I knew his answer before he spoke. "If we must," he finally said.

I felt sick to my stomach even considering the possibility of turning Earth into something resembling the first colony we had visited. I wasn't sure if I could let him do it. The rational part of my mind knew it might have to be done—for the greater good— but the emotional part of me loved that planet and the people who inhabited it, and I couldn't imagine a single situation where I wouldn't fight to save Earth.

"Well then," Artemis said, "I wish you luck, but I am sorry to tell you that we cannot help you. Our own ark ship must remain here as our last resort, should the Tsakali find us. Now, you must go. Your bridge has shattered the time dilation field, and we cannot reestablish it until the bridge is closed."

Hades bowed his head. "We will leave and close the bridge." He raised his head part of the way, spearing Artemis with his icy stare. "So long as you promise me one thing."

Artemis eyed her brother skeptically, "What *one thing*?"

"Do you have the ability to create clones here?" Hades asked.

Artemis nodded.

"Then we require cloned embryos in individual cryopods," Hades said. "I will return to pick them up once we've secured an ark ship."

I stared at him with widened eyes. This could be our people's fresh start—new, uninfected bodies. I had no idea how Hades would pull off transferring our people into the new bodies without infecting them with the nano-virus, but clearly, he thought there was a way.

Artemis considered the request for a long moment. "How many?"

"As many as you can create in the time between now and when I return," Hades told her.

Artemis turned partway, addressing the other Amazons through a psychic link. I could sense the link, if not the information being conveyed upon it. A moment later, one of the warriors spun around and ran off, presumably delivering a message for Artemis.

Artemis returned her attention to Hades. "You will have your clones. But for now, you must leave."

"Many thanks, little sister," Hades said dryly.

Artemis bowed her head.

Without another word, Hades turned his back to his long-lost sister and headed for the open bridge. I only hesitated for a moment before scooping up my doru and following.

I couldn't believe I had just met Artemis, one of the most renowned Amazon warriors of all time. I couldn't believe she was still alive, not as a clone, but as the original. And I really couldn't believe what a complete and utter disappointment she had turned out to be.

I emerged from the gephyra onto a hill in the center of a small Olympian settlement with half-built towers encapsulated in a thick, gleaming layer of ice. The ground was blanketed by snow, and fluffy snowflakes fell from the overcast sky in gentle flurries. My breath came out in a white puff of air and my cheeks and nose stung from the cold, and I was grateful for the hoplon suit's climate-control feature, keeping me from freezing my toes off.

At first, I thought Hades had made a mistake and formed a bridge back to Earth. Except, the Alpha site had been nearly completely unfrozen by the time we left. Plus, the dome of ice surrounding the energy barrier that protected the city blocked any view of the sky. This was someplace new.

"Come on through, guys," I said, walking around the gephyra to survey the unfinished city. The land surrounding this hill was remarkably flat, with rolling hills in the distance leading to jagged mountains that reached incredibly high into the sky. A few of the smaller towers spread throughout the settlement were complete, but most stood with their interiors exposed to the elements. It was as though the Olympians who had come here had started the colonization process but abandoned it before it was finished.

A large white mound barely visible between a couple of half-built towers just beyond the far edge of the city caught my eye, and I squinted to focus. It might have been a small, isolated hill, like the one I was currently standing on, but I was fairly certain I could sense the faintest tingle of energy coming from exactly that direction. That tingle stood out more than usual, surrounded by the utter deadness of the rest of the city.

I closed my eyes and focused on the tingle. The sensation strengthened under the full focus of my psychic senses, sending a thrill of excitement cascading over my skin. The mound wasn't a hill, but a dome-shaped energy shield, covered in ice. A protective barrier, like the one emitted from the central tower in the Alpha site, was there to protect the city from the ice cap threatening to consume it. It had to be.

My people erected energy barriers to protect one of two things—a settlement, or a ship. The dome was huge, but clearly not large enough to cover a settlement, considering I was standing in the local settlement and not remotely close to the dome. Which meant it had to be protecting a ship. And based on the size of the mound, it was a massive ship. Something like, oh say, an ark ship.

The sound of footsteps behind me alerted me to one of my companions' approach. I had been too distracted by my discovery to notice the arrival of his and the others' minds. I opened my eyes and glanced over my shoulder to see Raiden walking toward me.

"This doesn't look all that promising," he said, coming to stand beside me. His discouragement and frustration seeped in even though I had muted my psychic senses as much as possible where he and the others were concerned. "Another dead end?"

"I don't think so," I said, unable to keep the excitement from my voice, and looked past him. "Hey, Hades . . ." I raised one hand to wave the Olympian prince over. When he joined us, I pointed to the mound of ice at the edge of the unfinished settlement. "Think that mound is large enough to conceal an ark ship?"

Hades squinted. "Perhaps," he murmured. "Though it is hard to say from this distance."

I grinned at him. "Well then, don't you think we should get a closer look?" I could feel Hades' excitement rising to meet mine.

We didn't even bother splitting up the group. All together, we trekked through the frozen ghost town, and the closer we drew to the icy mound, the stronger the energy signature became. I grew increasingly certain that the mound of ice was, in fact, covering an energy dome. And it was absolutely enormous.

I jogged ahead, and when I reached the edge of the mound, I sheathed my doru and placed my hands flat against the frozen surface. Closing my eyes, I channeled a steady stream of psychic energy out through my hands, sending superheated tendrils branching throughout the ice, until it was all melted.

"Holy Mother of . . .," Fiona murmured.

I opened my eyes and took a step back from the exposed energy barrier, lowering my hands. An enormous ship shaped like a bullet lay beyond the shimmering silver barrier. The four largest skyscrapers on Earth could have been tipped on their sides and stuffed inside, and then some. The ship was practically a city all on its own. A slow grin spreading across my face, I turned to Hades, who I sensed standing at my right. His features were transformed by an expression of wonder.

"Well?" my mom said from my left. "Is it an ark ship?"

A laugh bubbled up my throat. It wasn't just an ark ship. It was the *Elysium*, a *grand* ark ship, capable of carrying billions of souls in miniature consciousness orbs, about the size of a shooter marble, and millions of frozen embryos. Like all ark ships, this one could sustain the "passengers" indefinitely, so long as the ship was powered by a chaos stone not taxed by frequent use of the FTL engine. The *Elysium*'s AI was the most advanced ever created by Olympians, able to initiate and direct the colonization and repopulation process on a new world all on its own once a suitable planet was found—or to assist when manually directed by a living, breathing crew.

"Yes," I said, grinning like a fool. "Yes, it most definitely is an ark ship."

Hades raised his forearm and activated the screen on his holoband. He swiped to the left, and then to the right, tapped the holographic screen a few times, and the silver energy barrier fizzled out.

I looked from Hades to my mom and Fiona. "You guys wait here." I shifted my focus to Raiden, standing on the other side of Hades. "Raiden and I will check it out and let you guys know if it's safe to come aboard."

Raiden nodded, his hand going to the laser pistol holstered on his hip.

"Do you think there could be live Olympians in there?" my mom asked.

I stared at the ship and chewed on the inside of my cheek, excitement warring with a sudden spike of uncertainty within me. Someone had activated the energy barrier that had been protecting the ship, and I didn't think it was the people who had abandoned the city before finishing it. Why would they have fled onto the ark ship, but not left the planet? That didn't make any sense.

I glanced over my shoulder, scanning the unfinished cityscape. What happened to these people? I turned back to the ship. And who activated the energy barrier? And when?

"Let's just say I don't *not* expect to find live Olympians on that ship . . . especially after what we found on the last planet," I admitted, and a combination of anxiety and excitement surged in the three humans.

"An energy shield can remain active indefinitely," Hades told them. "Once established, it requires a low but steady energy input to be maintained. This energy shield could have been established thousands of years ago."

"Or yesterday," I countered, then glanced at my mom, sensing her mounting eagerness to explore the ship, as well as Fiona's hunger to analyze the alien tech. "Just, wait here. Raiden and I will check it out, and then you guys can come aboard." I looked at Raiden, my eyes locking with his. "Ready?"

Raiden nodded and stepped forward. "Ready."

We climbed down over the eight-foot ledge of snow where the energy barrier had been and landed on dark, rich soil. In warmer weather, this land would have been perfect for agriculture. I could see why the Olympians who had started the colony here had chosen this location.

We headed for the *Elysium*, and as we approached, I psychically hacked into the ship's operating system. The AI was dormant, which didn't bode well for the prospect of finding a chaos stone on board. Had the ship been at full power, I could have linked with the AI like any other mind—a much easier task. But it wasn't, suggesting the ship was currently being powered by a power core instead. We could run the ship without a chaos stone, but we wouldn't be able to access the FTL drive, which meant it would take several thousand years to reach Earth, rather than several days. In that case, the ship would essentially be useless to us.

Concentrating, I navigated my way through the ship's complex systems to the manual controls and willed the nearest passenger hatch to open. A panel in the ship's hull slid open directly in front of us, and a long ramp extended down to the ground. I led the way up the ramp, my boots striking the metal surface like a gong with each step. As we neared the top of the ramp, the airlock chamber lit up, and I flashed back to all the times I had come and gone from the *Tartarus* during our first dozen or so years on Earth before the Alpha site had been completed.

Raiden and I paused in the airlock while I concentrated on the inner door. The metal panel slid open with a whoosh, emitting a hiss of stale air.

I exchanged a glance with Raiden, who drew his laser pistol, and then I marched through the open doorway and into the ship.

The corridor beyond was shaped like a trapezoid, just like in the *Tartarus*, with steel grating on the floors and polished steel on the walls and ceiling, reinforced by posts and beams of orichalcum alloy. The *Tartarus* had been an ark ship, and I was operating off the assumption that the layout of the *Elysium* was generally the same, just on a larger scale.

Raiden and I had boarded the ship on the main level, and we followed the entry corridor past numerous bisecting hallways to the wider central corridor, which if I was right about the layout of the *Elysium*, should run the length of the ship, connecting the engine rooms at the rear to the command center at the front.

"Seems like you know where you're going," Raiden commented as we hurried up the central corridor, our eyes constantly moving and weapons at the ready.

"Seems like it," I agreed, flashing him a nervous smile. "*Seems* being the operative word."

He chuckled.

"We'll find out if I actually *do* know where I'm going as soon as we're close enough to read the writing on those doors," I added, nodding toward the oversized double door panel ahead in the distance. If the blue, blocky letters spelled out the Olympian equivalent of *BRIDGE*, then my instincts would prove to be correct. If not, we would need to do some scouting to find the ship's command center.

Turned out, I had been right about the ship's layout. The bridge doors slid apart, revealing a vast chamber with a high, arched ceiling, completely empty save for the gephyra platform at the center of the floor and the curved control panel set off to the side. Like the corridor that had brought us here, the floor within the chamber was steel grating, the walls and ceiling polished steel reinforced by ribs of orichalcum alloy. At the far end of the chamber, a railing blocked the drop off to the open level below, and in either corner, a staircase curved down to the lower level of the bridge.

I crossed to the staircase on the right and hurried down the stairs to the ship's command center. Bypassing countless control stations, I headed for the captain's station on its raised pedestal further back in the room. I climbed up the steps and slid into the captain's chair, pressing a button on the desk in front of me to activate the holoscreen while Raiden looked around. I tapped the screen once, initiating a complete systems check, then swiped through a few menus to run a couple of ship-wide scans—the first for active life-forms, and the second specifically for Tsakali.

Within seconds, a box popped up on the holoscreen displaying a 3D cross-section of the bullet-shaped ship, and two tiny blue dots blinked near the ship's snubbed nose. Raiden and I were the only living things here. A second box popped up beside the first, reporting that zero Tsakali life-forms had been detected.

"Alright guys," I said through the comms patch, "come on in. We're in the command center." While we waited for the others to join us, I ran a third scan, this time for chaos signatures.

A new box popped up on the screen, again displaying a cross-section of the ship, and a vertical green line slowly moved from the tail end of the ship toward the front, representing the progress of the current scan.

"Does every Olympian ship have a gephyra?" Raiden asked,

heading my way. He glanced up at the ceiling like he could see the gephyra through the layers of steel.

"Every ark ship," I told him, watching the slow progress of the green line on the screen. "Plus, they usually carry an extra gephyra in storage for the colony itself."

A faint, blinking green dot appeared on the diagram of the ship, directly above us, in the gephyra chamber, signifying that the scan had detected a weak chaos signature. I had expected it, but not the ping that appeared a moment later. A second green dot blinked a level below us, almost directly in line with the first dot, but even fainter.

"That's strange," I said as I sat up straighter, reaching out to zoom in on the diagram. I rotated the diagram to get a better idea of what I was looking at.

Raiden climbed the steps to the captain's pedestal and joined me. "What is it?" he asked, standing to the left of my chair.

"I ran a search for chaos signatures and got two hits, but the readings don't make sense." I pointed to the stronger of the two blinking green dots, clearly indicating that the chaos signature was coming from the gephyra. "That's the gephyra above us," I told Raiden, briefly glancing at the ceiling. "It's powered by chaos fragments."

Raiden's confusion seeped into me.

I could hear footsteps on metal overhead and sensed the others' minds approaching.

"Think of chaos fragments like mini chaos stones," I told him. "Like a watch battery compared to a car battery."

Raiden nodded slowly. "Alright."

Hades descended the stairs from the level above first, followed by my mom and Fiona, who scanned this new space with wide, awe-filled eyes. When Hades reached the floor of the command center, he made a beeline for us.

I returned my attention to the holoscreen, pointing to the second, weaker blinking green dot. "This one is a level below us," I said. "In the cryovault, but what's weird is that this signature is even weaker than that of the chaos fragments above us."

"It could be a single fragment," Hades offered, climbing the steps to the captain's station. He settled in on my right.

I narrowed my eyes, studying the diagram, and shook my head. "But why would a single chaos fragment be down there?"

"Or," Hades said, "it could be a containment box muting the signature of a chaos stone."

Cold washed over me, and I went absolutely, completely still. For seconds, I didn't even breathe. I sensed that Hades' thoughts had gone to the same place as mine—to the team of Amazons who had found a chaos stone while searching the lost colonies twelve thousand years ago and had been moments from reestablishing a bridge to return to Earth when Hades yanked the chaos fragments from the guts of the gephyra, thus stranding the team of Amazons off-world.

I exchanged a look with Hades, then stood and silently climbed down from the platform. I felt like I was moving through a dream as I approached the staircase tucked in the back right corner of the bridge.

"What?" I heard Raiden say behind me. I could sense both him and Hades following. "What is it?"

I ignored him, erecting mental blinders in my mind. My heart thudded in my throat, and my ribs closed in around my lungs, making it harder to breathe. I had a single purpose—to go down into the cryovault and find the source of the chaos signature . . . and to see if any of the cryochambers were occupied. An occupied cryochamber wouldn't have pinged the life-form scan, so it was a very real possibility that the team of Amazons was down there, cryogenically frozen, just waiting for someone to wake them.

I descended the spiraling steel staircase into the cryovault, and lights flared on overhead, illuminating row after row of cryochambers on either side of the elongated space. A containment box sat on the floor in front of the third cryochamber on the right side of the cryovault. I froze at the foot of the stairs, my eyes drawn past the containment box to the cryochamber behind it.

And to the mummified corpse of the Amazon warrior who had died within.

[20]

"A containment box!" Hades exclaimed from the stairs behind me. He gripped my shoulders, the contact allowing his glee at finding another chaos stone to overflow into me. "We did it, Cora. We can save them. We can take this ship back to Earth and . . ." His words trailed off as shock replaced his glee. He had seen the body in the cryochamber behind the containment box, my worst fear come to life.

I pulled free from his weak grasp and slowly approached the cryochamber, passing the containment box and coming to stand directly in front of the desecrated corpse of one of my spearsisters, only a thick pane of glass separating us. Her skin was blackened by age and as thin as paper, her eye sockets were empty black holes, and her lower jaw hung partially unhinged, locking her in an eternal scream. It was impossible to identify which of the five Amazon warriors Hades and I had stranded here I was looking at, but there were only five options. Five women I had known for centuries. Five women I have trained and fought alongside. Five women I had, to varying degrees, considered friends. Now that my fear had been realized, it washed away under waves of sorrow and guilt.

Reciting their names in my head—Mnemosyne, Phoebe, Selene, Metis, and Nike—I placed my palm against the glass. No hint of cold touched my skin, as it should have, had the cryosystem been functioning properly.

Licking my lips, I opened my mouth to speak, but found I had no voice, so I cleared my throat and tried again. "Hades," I said, my voice sounding hollow, "run a diagnostic on the cryosystem."

"Running it now," he confirmed. He was behind me, standing near the containment box, from the sound of his voice, accessing the ship's systems through his holoband. "Is it—is it them?"

"Yes," I breathed, suffocating under the guilt and grief of having caused this horrific outcome.

"Cryosystem diagnostic complete," Hades informed me. "I'm seeing five occupied cryochambers." He paused for a moment. "All have failed save for one."

I closed my eyes and bowed my head, a tear streaking down my cheek as I mourned my fallen spearsisters. "Which one?"

"Cryochamber seven."

I took a deep breath, raised my head and opened my eyes, and turned my back to the cryochamber holding my dead spearsister. I crossed to the opposite side of the cryovault, tracking the numbers inscribed at the top of each cryochambers until I reached *seven*. Holding my breath, I tore my eyes from the number overhead to peer through the glass to the face beyond. Selene.

My heart surged with relief. Of the five Amazon warriors we had stranded here, Selene had been my closest friend. She looked perfect, her pale, moonlight skin unblemished, and her eyes closed in cryosleep.

"Do you want me to initiate the wake sequence?" Hades asked me.

I drew in a breath to say yes, but hesitated, thinking through the ramifications of waking Selene right now. I would have to explain the situation. It would take time and effort, and we still had so much to do to get this ship in the air and on its way to Earth.

"Not yet," I said, turning to face Hades, still standing beside the containment box. "Has the systems check completed yet?"

Hades looked from me to the screen hovering above his holoband and back. The screen of his holoband displayed a replica of the larger holoscreen at the captain's station on the floor above us. "Ninety-three percent," he told me.

I nodded to myself. "Let's wait on the results." I glanced at the cryochamber directly across from us. It contained another corpse.

There was a chance that running a successful wake sequence wasn't even possible right now, and I wasn't willing to have the blood of yet another of my spearsisters on my hands. Not if I could help it.

I started toward the spiraling staircase.

Raiden stood at the foot of the stairs, watching me, his eyes filled with concern. He moved to the side as I approached.

I paused when I reached him, my eyes meeting his, and my chin trembled.

He rested his hand on my shoulder, giving me a gentle squeeze. His expression told me he understood my pain. The grief. The guilt. The shame. He didn't say anything. He didn't need to.

I covered his hand with mine and flashed him a weak smile. And then I kept walking, making my way back up the spiral staircase to the command center.

A box popped up on the holoscreen at the captain's station as I approached. The ship-wide systems check was complete.

I jogged ahead, racing up the steps of the pedestal to the captain's station, and reclaimed the chair. I tapped on the pop-up, and it vanished, replaced by another, larger box listing the ship's various systems. All were grayed out, indicating they were offline, except for the mainframe, life support, and the cryosystem, the last of which blinked red, announcing a critical failure.

Hades joined me at the captain's station, the containment box tucked against his side under his arm.

"Can you tell what's causing the cryosystem failure?" I asked him, leaning forward as he reached out to swipe across the screen with his free hand.

Hades navigated through a series of menus, then pulled up detailed readouts from several systems. He swiped them all away, leaving only the readings from the mainframe. "The entire ship is running on the backup power core," he said, shaking his head in disgust. It was too close for comfort to the situation at the Omega site back home. "The other cryochambers likely would have been fine if the shield hadn't been erected around the ship," he thought aloud, "but over time, it must have drawn too much power, draining the power core completely and depleting the backup." He breathed deeply. "Our arrival hasn't helped, drawing power to the lights and ship infrastructure . . ."

I swallowed my mounting fear and looked up at Hades. "How long until the final cryochamber fails?"

Hades' eyes met mine. "At the most, days. At the least, hours."

"Could we rig the ship to run off the chaos stone instead of a power core?"

Hades shook his head. "Our ships weren't built with inter-changeable power receivers like in our cities. The chaos stone powers the FTL drive and the AI system, and the power core handles everything else. If we tried to replace the power core with a chaos stone, we would fry the entire ship."

I held his stare for a long moment. We had a chaos stone. We could plug it into the column in the city's mainframe and produce a new power core, but it would take a while. I thought back to the power core we had found in the desert colony. We were already producing a new power core for the Omega site down in the Alpha site's mainframe, leaving the scavenged power core unallocated. I nodded to myself, certain I had found the perfect solution.

"Raiden," I said through the comms patch, standing as I scanned the command center in search of him. I couldn't see him anywhere. "Where are you?"

He appeared in the back corner, climbing up the spiral staircase from the cryovault below.

"I need you to run back to the gephyra and retrieve that power core we found in the desert colony," I told him as he approached the captain's pedestal.

"You got it." He changed trajectory and jogged toward the stairs up to the gephyra chamber.

I turned to Hades. "If we replace the power core, could the ship run?"

Hades pulled up the detailed report from the systems check, narrowing his eyes as he skimmed the information. "I don't see why not," he finally said. "All systems are in good shape. The only thing causing problems is the failing power core."

I nodded to myself. "How long would it take to reach Earth from here?"

"With the chaos stone to power the FTL drive . . ." He swiped the holoscreen clear and pulled up the navigation pane, quickly programming in Earth's coordinates. "Three Earth days," he finally said.

"That's what we'll do then," I told him. "As soon as Raiden returns with the power core, we'll get the ship up and running. Once we're en route to Earth, we'll wake Selene and explain the situation."

I sensed Hades was bearing the burden of causing the other four Amazons' deaths about as well as I was, trying not to drown under the tsunami of guilt. I stood and touched his arm, offering him a weak smile of understanding. Whatever happened between us in the future, this guilt would link us forever.

When Hades' eyes met mine, I gave his arm a squeeze. "If we hadn't done it, they all would have died anyway," I told him gently. "We never could have outrun the Tsakali. They were too close. We did what had to be done—sacrificed a few to save the many."

Hades closed his eyes and bowed his head, covering my hand with his. "They were good people. Their lives mattered." He raised his head and looked at me with red-rimmed eyes, and this rare moment of vulnerability sent fissures through my heart. "I don't know how much longer I can do this. How many more have to die?" He swallowed roughly. "Will this fight never end?"

I leaned in, drawn in by the rawness of his pain, and rested my forehead against his. "We'll keep going for as long as we can," I told him. Promised him. "We'll keep fighting, together, until it's over." Either we would win, or we would lose. But we wouldn't quit. We wouldn't give up. We would never give up because then all the pain and loss and death and sacrifice would have been for nothing.

With a sigh, I pulled away. My stare locked with Hades', and after a long moment, he nodded.

I rested my hand on his cheek, just for a heartbeat, and then I turned away from him and climbed down from the captain's station, heading for my mom and Fiona. They stood together near the front of the command center, studying the star map on a holoscreen that hovered over the navigation control panel. I explained the situation to them, then returned to the captain's pedestal.

An hour later—after no word from Raiden—I was growing antsy. He should have made it through the gephyra and back to this planet by now.

"Raiden?" I said through the comms patch. "What's the status on the power core?"

There was no response.

"Raiden?" I repeated, standing from my perch on the arm of the captain's chair. "Emi?" Still nothing. "Hello?" I exchanged a nervous look with Hades, who now occupied the captain's chair as he poured over the detailed reports from the systems check.

He pulled up the screen on his holoband, and I could feel his dread before he announced, "The bridge to Earth has closed."

My muscles tensed, and I clenched my jaw. That explained why Raiden and Emi weren't responding. Our own communications weren't getting through.

"Should we be worried?" my mom asked.

I shook my head. "These things happen—random bursts of energy can disrupt the bridge, and the longer a bridge is open, the more likely something like this is to happen."

Hades tapped the holoscreen several times, then frowned. "I must be closer to the gephyra to establish another bridge."

"Can't we just use the one up there?" my mom asked, pointing up to the level above us as she approached the captain's station.

Hades shook his head. "Unfortunately, no. A permanent gephyra established on a planet always overrides a ship-bound gephyra."

I blew out a breath, attempting to dispel some of his dread. Mine was plenty enough. "All right," I said. "Let's head back to Earth. We'll need supplies for the trip anyway."

The group was quiet as we trekked back through the snow to the gephyra on the hill at the center of the unfinished settlement. Tensions mounted the closer we drew. Why had the bridge collapsed? And more importantly, why hadn't Emi attempted to establish a new one?

As we trudged up the hill, I sensed a presence lurking behind a frozen tree off to my right, near the base of the hill. Not human, and not Olympian, but definitely sentient. I spun that way, simultaneously charging and aiming my doru.

But before I could get a lock on it—whatever it was—it bolted. My eyes bugged out as I watched the lurker scamper off. It was humanoid, and small, dressed in a full-body suit of some thick, silver-gray fabric. And if I wasn't mistaken, it was a child.

[21]

"Cora!" Hades hissed. "You cannot let it get away!"

My stare snapped to him, just for a fraction of a second, and his spike of fear shocked me out of stunned inaction. Without another thought, I sprinted down the hill, chasing after the child-like lurker loping away.

It was fast, but its legs were short, and it moved with an increasingly pronounced limp. I was faster. Once I was within five yards of the creature, I skidded to a stop and rammed the butt of my doru into the snow. An electric-blue energy barrier burst up out of the ground ahead of my quarry, trapping it with me in an impenetrable circle.

Cautiously, the creature reached out to the barrier with one hand. It hissed the moment it made contact, stung by the electri-fied energy, and cowered on the frozen ground.

I stalked closer, attempting to dig into its mind to discover its purpose here and to figure out its language, but I couldn't glean anything beyond a vague sense of fear and pain.

It raised its face to me.

I halted mid-step and muttered, "What the hell?"

It *was* a child. An Olympian child—a young girl—from the

looks of it, though how that was possible, I couldn't begin to imagine. This place was half-finished and long abandoned. For an Olympian child to be present, there needed to be active cloning happening.

Moving slowly, so as not to spook the girl any further, I sheathed my doru on my back and took a step closer to her, then another. I held my hands out where the girl could see them, attempting to put her at ease. "Hey . . ." I kept my voice soft, gentle. "I'm not going to hurt you. Are you all right? What are you doing out here?"

The girl whimpered and hid her face behind her raised knees.

In the back of my mind, I knew something was off. It didn't make sense for a lone Olympian child to be here. But still, I moved closer.

The others reached the outside of my energy barrier, and Hades banged against the sheet of energy, ignoring the electrified sting. "Back away from that thing, Cora!" he shouted. "It is incredibly dangerous!"

I stopped and glanced at him, brows knitting together in confusion. Alarm flashed across his face, partially obscured by the shimmering barrier. I turned back to the child and found it had transformed into a monster, with bulging veins, red-rimmed irises, and steel fangs and claws.

Heart hammering, I stumbled back a few steps.

The hell-child lunged at me.

I barely had time to react, tumbling backward and kicking the creature over me as I rolled. I drew my doru as I regained my feet and sent out a stunning blast.

The hell-child dropped to the snow-covered ground, uncon-scious. Its steel claws retracted, and the protruding veins settled back in its skin. Once again, it appeared to be an innocent Olympian child.

Breathing hard and keeping my doru aimed at the *thing*, I lowered the energy barrier, letting the others through. "What the hell is it?" I asked Hades as he ran over, my mom and Fiona close on his heels.

Hades slowed to a jog, then stopped beside me and stared down at the stunned creature. "A Tsakali scout," he said between heaving breaths. "They model their shells after what the children of their kind once looked like to make them appear unassuming and vulnerable."

"I'd say it worked," I grumbled.

The Tsakali scout stirred, and I charged the doru's focus crystal, intending to deliver a killing blow before it could recover enough to attack us.

Hades reached out, resting his hand on the staff and pushing the aim of the focus crystal off to the side. "Don't kill it just yet. If we bring it back to Earth alive, we can use it to demonstrate the true nature of the Tsakali to the human leaders. Perhaps then, they will understand the danger."

I looked at Hades, uncertain. This thing was dangerous; the prospect of it escaping and delivering its intel catastrophic. It needed to be destroyed.

But standing so close, and with my own mental barriers lagging, it was impossible not to skim some of Hades' surface thoughts. This *thing* might be just what we needed to convince the humans of Earth to destroy all record of the chaos stone and how it was created. It might be our only way to save them from us and what we would have to do if they refused.

I turned my attention back to the Tsakali scout but let the charge fade from the doru's focus crystal. Heaving out a breath, I sheathed my doru and pointed to the scout with my chin. "Hold its arms behind its back," I said. "I want it restrained before it's fully awake."

Hades crouched down beside the scout, and my mom stepped forward to join him. They rolled the scout onto its side and pressed its wrists together, and I wound thin, unbreakable ropes of energy around its wrists. The bindings would hold, so long as I had access to my psychic gifts.

My mom added military-grade zip ties, just in case, and slapped a couple of strips of duct tape over its mouth for good measure. She pulled an empty sack out of her pack and covered its head, then helped Hades haul the groggy scout up to its feet.

Hands on my hips, I studied their handiwork and nodded. "Good enough. Let's head back to the gephyra. I'll feel better once we can get this thing locked in a cage."

Hades led the way back to the gephyra, my mom and me hauling the scout between us. As soon as we reached the gephyra, Hades established a new bridge to Earth.

"On our way back, Em," my mom said through the comms patch. When Emi didn't respond, my mom's worried gaze locked with mine. "Em? Are you there?"

"Raiden?" I said. "Can you hear us?"

But still, there was no response. We exchanged wary looks all around.

I stepped forward, leaving the scout in my mom's hands, and climbed up the first step of the gephyra platform. Dread knotted in my gut, and I paused to look back at the others. "Wait for me to give the all clear."

Fiona stared at me with wide, unblinking eyes.

My mom nodded.

Hades' expression was guarded, but I sensed that he was unwilling to agree. If he thought I was truly in danger, he would dive across the bridge and do whatever he could to help.

I knew arguing with him would get me nowhere, so I sighed and turned back to the giant, quicksilver orb marking the entrance to the bridge home. Once the focus crystal of my doru was charged, I plunged across the bridge.

And stepped into a scene taken straight out of a nightmare.

Emi and Raiden sat on the floor in front of the curved control panel, their arms bound behind their backs and their ankles tied together. Two heavily armed commando types guarded them, the silver emblem on their black armored vests marking them as soldiers of the Custodes Veritatis.

Meg knelt off to the side of the control panel, restrained in much the same way, a golden Amazon collar snug around her neck, suppressing her psychic powers. Twice as many Order soldiers guarded her.

And then there was Henry Magnusson, standing behind the control panel, his arms crossed over his chest and a malicious grin curving his lips. "Welcome back, ancient one."

I aimed the charged doru at Henry, but before I could fire a killing blast, warm metal encircled my neck and latched with a resonant *click*. The electric-blue glow faded from the grooves running the length of the doru, and then from the focus crystal as my psychic powers winked out.

They had been waiting for me to return. They had been ready, and I had been so distracted, I had let them collar me.

"Cora?" my mom said, her voice transmitted across the open bridge through my comms patch.

I spun around, striking at the woman who had collared me with the dormant doru. She tumbled backward, falling onto her butt, and I knocked her out with a swing of the doru to her chin. I brought down three more Order soldiers, but soon I found myself surrounded, at least a dozen assault rifles aimed at me. At full power, my hoplon suit would have protected me from their bullets, even at such close range. The impact of each bullet still would have stung, but I wouldn't have been harmed beyond a little bruising. Now, however, there were no guarantees.

I crouched, my doru clutched in both hands, and slowly turned in a circle to assess the situation. It didn't look good for me.

"Cora?" my mom repeated. "What's going on?"

I didn't dare respond. Doing so might clue in Henry and his

minions to the fact that the bridge worked both ways, and then they would cross over and capture my mom and the others.

As things stood now, at least my mom, Hades, and Fiona were still free. They could use the other chaos stone to produce a new power core in the frozen city's mainframe, then travel back here in the ark ship and break us free. I wasn't sure of Selene's prospects, but there wasn't much I could do about that right now.

With a *whoosh*, my mom emerged from the gephyra, her laser pistol drawn. Hades followed, dragging the scout with one hand, laser pistol brandished in the other. Fiona came last, her own laser pistol grasped in her trembling hand. But all their weapons were a drop of water in an ocean compared to the fire-power Henry's veritable army was aiming our way.

I bowed my head and dropped the doru. It clanged on the floor at my feet, then slowly rolled away as I fell to my knees in surrender.

[22]

I sat on the floor in the middle of a room that had once been a private office high up in the central tower of the Alpha site, some twelve thousand years ago. The room was small, maybe ten feet by ten feet, and had been cleared of all furniture and decor, leaving behind a faintly musty smell. The narrow window in the exterior wall provided my only access to the outside world, but it was useless to me. I couldn't even dive to my death hundreds of feet below. The glass was reinforced, unbreakable to me in my powerless state.

I couldn't believe I had let this happen again. Let myself be a prisoner again. Over twelve millennia had passed since I was last held prisoner in this place. That had been the beginning of the end, mere hours before my death. It hadn't mattered that I had escaped . . . that Hades and I had come together to do what needed to be done to save this planet. My sacrifice then had been necessary.

I couldn't help but wonder what I might have to sacrifice this time. I feared the planet was doomed, but there was still time to save the handful of people I loved. It was better than nothing.

Growling under my breath, I pounded the side of my fist against the floor.

Why did it feel like I was stuck in a loop? Like no matter how hard I tried, it would always come down to this—to the Tsakali threatening my people, and to those in power thwarting my efforts to save them? It was like the universe was one giant record player, but the record was scratched, and we were stuck acting out the same struggle, over and over again. Whether I was Peri or Cora or the strange hybrid of the two I had become, it was always the same. I'd been in this exact same position all those millennia ago, but it felt like it was only yesterday.

With another growl of frustration, I stood up and paced around the small room. I was tired of sitting on my butt, doing nothing. I'd been stuck in here for hours, and wallowing was getting me nowhere. I had promised Hades I would keep fighting, and I had meant it. Maybe I wasn't in prime Amazon shape at the moment, but I was still me—Peri, Cora, *me*—and I could find a way out of this.

I stopped in front of the window and stared down at the Order minions skittering about far below, moving from building to building as they plundered this once glorious city. Henry was getting what he wanted—unhindered access to our tech. Not that he would have any idea of how to use it. My only solace was in knowing that Hades would never spill the location of the Omega site. He would never deliver the last remains of our people over to our enemy, no matter what the Order did to him.

I raised my hands to my neck and tugged at the metal collar. If only I had access to my powers, I would be able to squash Henry and his minions like the cockroaches they were. But as things currently stood, there were far too many Order soldiers for me to take on alone, even if I somehow managed to break out of my prison.

Again, I thought back to those final hours before my last

death. I had awakened in a prison cell, collared and powerless, and I had broken free.

There was a way. I knew I could get the stupid collar off. I'd done it once before. But it would take time and concentration . . . and a whole lot of calm. Everyone I loved was currently being held prisoner somewhere else in the Alpha site. It wasn't exactly a calm-inducing situation.

I planted my hands on the wall to either side of the window and leaned in, resting my forehead against the unbreakable glass. The Peri part of me felt defeated, but the Cora part of me—the gamer part of me—wanted to attack the seemingly impossible challenge head-on.

Exhaling heavily, I pushed away from the window and stalked to the center of the room. I lowered myself down onto the floor and sat cross-legged, closing my eyes and taking deep, belly breaths, like Emi had taught me to do years ago during my first few yoga lessons. I focused on the physical act of breathing, on the sensation of my lungs expanding and contracting. On the individual beats of my heart and the thrum of blood rushing through my veins. On the small, minor aches and pains left over from the fight in the gephyra chamber.

And slowly—ever so slowly—my rage and misery faded. But they weren't replaced by calm, as had been my goal. They were replaced by someone else's emotions. Someone else's misery and fear. It took me a moment to recognize the emotions as belonging to Meg.

My eyes snapped open, my concentration shattering.

Meg. I had forgotten about Meg. Well, I hadn't forgotten about her, exactly, but I'd neglected my connection to her. I'd been so pissed off about being captured that I hadn't sensed her emotions seeping into me through our tamped down bond. While the collar was suppressing my psychic powers, it looked like it couldn't touch our bond.

I closed my eyes again and focused on the invisible thread

that connected me to Meg, opening up to it. Welcoming it. Accepting it. Ever since our bond was created, I had been so intent on stifling the connection that I hadn't realized just how much effort I was expending doing just that. Tensions I hadn't been aware of relaxed as the bond between us flowed freely.

The full force of Meg's emotions flooded into me, along with her surface thoughts and a general sense of her surroundings. The connection felt *right*, and I no longer understood why I had been fighting it so hard.

Meg was being held in the ancient Olympian version of a conference room, the space stripped of all furnishings, just like my prison. The others were with her, including the childlike Tsakali scout. I frowned, thinking Henry and his lackeys must not have figured out who—or rather, *what*—the scout really was yet. He probably thought she was just another Olympian and planned on dealing with her later.

Meg and the others were no longer bound, which was a relief. Still, seeing them all imprisoned like that relit the rage within me at being captured, and I found myself more determined than ever to break out of my collar and escape. I wanted nothing more than to get them—and me—way the hell out of here, away from the man who was hellbent on forging a path that would not only destroy this planet, but may very well doom the entire universe.

We needed to escape. And then we needed to end Henry Magnusson.

Before he ended *everything*.

"Meg?" I said, speaking aloud in the empty room as I projected my thoughts through the tether binding us together. "Can you hear me?"

I knew she had sensed the change in our bond. I could feel recognition and excitement snuffing out her misery and fear. But I had never tried to communicate with her directly through our bond before, and I wasn't even sure if it would work.

"Yes!" Meg exclaimed, her voice both audible and not. "I can hear you!" Confusion trickled across the bond. "Where are you? I can't tell . . ."

"I'm being held on one of the upper floors of the central tower," I told her. "Where are you?"

"We're on the fourth floor," Meg said. "That's why I couldn't get a sense of your location—you're too far away."

I nodded to myself. I could sense that Meg was much recovered from the taxing procedure that had cured her solar allergy, which was reassuring, but I couldn't glean much from Meg's surface thoughts about how the others were faring. Their capture hadn't involved much of a physical struggle, but there was no way to know what had been done to them after we'd been parted.

"How is everyone?" I asked. "Is anyone injured?"

"Only our pride," Meg said wryly.

I smiled to myself. I could relate. But despite the many —*many*—strikes my pride had taken over the past week, since the merging of my two selves, I finally felt like I was settling into my new identity. I felt comfortable with myself. Confident. Ready to kick some Order ass.

"I'm going to get out of here," I told Meg. "I'm going to get us all out of here, but I need your help."

Meg's reply was immediate. "Anything."

"I can remove the collar," I explained, "but I need to seek out a place of absolute calm and serenity within myself . . . and I can't get there if I have other emotions trickling in."

A rush of embarrassment flowed across the bond as Meg realized my meaning—that her emotions were holding me up.

"Do you know how to meditate?" I asked her.

I sensed Meg speaking with my mom, clarifying the meaning of the word *meditate*. "Yes," she finally said. "We learn focus exercises when we are very young. It helps us gain better control over our gifts."

I nodded to myself, figuring as much. It was a standard part of Amazon training, as well.

"Perfect," I said. "That's all I need you to do. Focus and be calm. I'm going to cinch our bond as tight as possible to minimize the flow of emotions between us, but I'll let you know as soon as I'm free." I was quiet for a moment, then added, "Tell the others to be ready."

"Of course." Meg fell quiet, though I could sense she had more to say. "But . . . where will we go?" she finally asked. "We cannot fight our way out of this."

"I'm not planning on fighting," I told her as I focused my thoughts on the gephyra and drew a mental picture of the frozen settlement and the *Elysium*, knowing Meg would sense the direction of my mind. I gave her the time she needed to piece together a solid understanding of my plan, and then I clamped down on our bond, minimizing our connection to the barest trickle.

Once again, I focused on my physical body. On my heartbeat. On my breathing. Inhale, exhale. Inhale, exhale. Inhale, exhale. And I settled into the calm.

[23]

I sat cross-legged on the floor in the middle of the office, high up in the central tower, my eyes closed and my breathing slow and steady. I floated in an ocean of calm, all my fears and worries drifting away around me. Only the present mattered. Only breathing. Only being.

It was a matter of hours and a matter of seconds. It took an eternity to get there, to reach the place of complete and utter calm within myself, but once I was there, psychic energy flooded into me, and the collar popped open, falling into my lap. It shouldn't have been possible. The Amazon collars had been designed back on Olympus to be inescapable, but that was back when all the Amazon warriors had been *born*. I was the only one who had been *made*. For some reason I didn't understand, that difference mattered.

I deactivated my regulator, then slouched my spine and let my head fall back, a giddy grin spreading across my face as I basked in the rush of psychic energy saturating my body. My nerves tingled with pleasure, and my synapses sang with joy.

Taking a deep breath, I straightened my neck and tossed the

collar into the corner of the room. If I'd had any inkling of how to destroy the damn thing, I would have. But it was made of orichalcum, rendering it effectively immune to psychic energy. I would have to ask Hades if there was a way to destroy the collars —he was the one who invented them, after all.

I unclamped the bond I shared with Meg and sensed that the young psychic was still deep in a meditative calm.

"Meg?" I murmured, not wanting to startle her.

Her awareness roused, and a spike of excitement surged through the bond from her to me. "You did it!" she exclaimed. I sensed her curiosity as she wondered if she might be able to break out of her collar, as well.

"I honestly don't know if you could do it," I told her. "It's not supposed to be possible—at least not for an Olympian—but I think because I was engineered and not born, something my creators coded into my DNA grants me elevated powers from the average natural-born Amazon warrior." I shrugged, thinking it would be worth asking Hades about at some point—later, when our lives, the planet, and the entire universe weren't at risk. "You can try to break free," I added, "but I'll be there to free you soon."

I sensed Meg's desire to make an attempt, but it warred with her internal commitment to ensure the others were prepared for their great escape.

"There's just one thing I need to take care of first," I told her, letting her sense my intent before clamping down on our bond once more. I couldn't afford any distractions for what I was about to do.

I stood and approached the room's lone door, stopping within arm's reach. I cast out my psychic radar and picked up on the mental signatures of two Order soldiers standing guard in the hallway on the other side of the door, one male, one female. Both capable warriors.

Deciding to take the subtle approach—better to draw as little attention to my escape as possible—I retreated to the corner of the room and sat down, hiding the discarded collar behind me. I pulled up my legs, hugging my knees, and ducked my head down to hide the lack of a golden collar encircling my neck.

With a focused thought, I unlocked the door and pulled it open, letting it swing inward a few inches, just enough to draw my guards' attention. Almost immediately, I sensed their confusion and wariness, and I feared they would call for backup.

Breath held, I listened to their hushed whispers out in the hallway as they discussed what to do. The corners of my mouth ticked upward as they played a quick round of Rock, Paper, Scissors to decide who would enter my prison cell first—without calling for backup.

A moment later, the door inched further open, and the female guard stepped into the room. I could feel her mind slowly moving closer to me. The male—the coward—hovered just outside the doorway.

I gritted my teeth, making myself wait for him.

Finally, he stepped into the room.

My head snapped up, and I slammed the door shut with a thought. Before they could reach for their radios, I stretched out my arm and sent a small psychic blast from my hand to stun them. The blast was more difficult to control without my doru, and I may have hit them a little harder than I had intended.

They flew backward, slamming against two different walls, then slid to the floor, unconscious. At least, I hoped they were only unconscious. I hated killing people who were only following orders. I had been in their shoes more times than I could count.

I scrambled up to my feet and hurried over to the woman, pressing my fingers against her neck. Her pulse was weak but steady. She would survive. I blew out a relieved breath, then quickly checked the guy before disarming both guards and collecting their radios, tossing everything into an office down the hall. I returned to bind their wrists and ankles with their own zip ties, then shut the door to the office and locked it with a focused thought.

Pausing in the hallway just outside the room that had been my prison cell, I closed my eyes, concentrating for a moment as I channeled psychic energy into my hoplon suit to activate its stealth mode. And then I was running. It was only a matter of time until more of the Order's soldiers discovered that my guards and I had traded places. I was racing against a clock, only I didn't know how much time I had.

I rushed down the endless spiraling steps, taking them two at a time but always paying attention. Always keeping a psychic eye out for the minds of my enemies in case I needed to slow down and sneak past. I raced down to the second floor and slipped into the gephyra chamber unnoticed.

The gephyra was still active, the quicksilver orb marking the opening of the bridge to the frozen settlement shining on its golden platform. That was excellent news for more than one reason. It meant we wouldn't have to wait for a new bridge to form when it was time to make our escape to that other world. But more importantly, it meant that Henry and his goons didn't know how to operate the gephyra's controls. Order scientists clustered around the control panel, their laptops out as they attempted to make sense of the machine. Their confusion and frustration clouded the room.

I smirked, pleased that something was finally going our way. Emi must have shut down the bridge when the Order first attacked because they certainly didn't know how to do it on their own. And if they couldn't even close a bridge, they certainly wouldn't be able to open one. Which meant they wouldn't be able to follow us when we fled.

Henry strode out from behind the gephyra, heading for the control panel. He had my doru on hand and was tapping it on the floor with every other step, like it was a powerful wizard's staff, when in reality, to him it was little more than a glitzy walking stick.

My smirk turned into a sneer. I wanted nothing more than to walk up to him, snatch my doru out of his hands, and impale him with the staff weapon. But we couldn't afford the shitstorm that would unleash right now. Cutting off the head of the snake might only clear the way for more to sprout.

Silently, I backed out of the gephyra chamber, then turned and ran back to the stairs. I continued my journey downward, heading into the sublevel beneath the ground floor, and found my way into the mainframe. The labyrinth of complex machines and control panels was swarming with Order scientists studying the alien equipment.

I snuck through the maze of machinery to the heart of the mainframe. The column in the center was untouched, and I wondered if the scientists had yet to figure out that the chaos stone was stowed within, hidden as it powered the city around them.

Moving on silent feet, I made my way closer to the power core generator situated off to the side of the central space. The generator was dormant, and I could see the brand-new power core Hades had ordered cradled in the machine's well. I reached into the well, and gripped either side of the power core, but hesitated before tugging it free.

Stealth mode wouldn't work here, not when I needed to actually interact with my environment. The four scientists dissecting the immediate vicinity may not have been able to see me, but one of these turds was bound to notice a power core floating on its own across the room.

This would require a different type of deception—a disguise rather than invisibility—but altering my appearance would require a massive output of psychic energy. I wasn't sure I wanted to exhaust myself here and now when I still needed to free the others and escort them safely through the gephyra.

I considered abandoning the power core, but then we would have to wait for the generator in the frozen settlement to create one—assuming it was even in working condition—and there was no saying how long it would take Henry's people to figure out the gephyra's controls. I couldn't risk them rebuilding the bridge and invading our refuge before we were able to get the *Elysium* up and running.

Making a split-second decision, I hurried out of the central clearing and ducked into a small side alcove, where I dropped out of stealth mode. I took a deep breath, then closed my eyes and concentrated on generating a widespread field of perception-altering psychic energy, just as I had done when I had disguised Fiona to sneak her into the Atlantea Project building. Anyone who looked at me from within the field's area of effect would see someone else entirely. They would see Henry Magnusson, the one person nobody would dare to question when he did something strange like, oh say, walk off with a power core for no apparent reason.

Disguise in place, I straightened my shoulders and donned an air of haughty, masculine entitlement, and then I marched back into the clearing at the heart of the mainframe like I owned the place.

I was noticed immediately, but only one of the scientists actually approached me, and he was easily put off with a silent glare. Sweat beaded on my brow as I retrieved the power core as quickly as possible. Hyper aware of the eyes on me, I tucked the power core under my arm and navigated my way out of the underground maze of machinery. I was five steps from the doorway to the hall that would take me back to the spiral staircase when the real Henry Magnusson strode through the doorway.

He froze, his eyes meeting mine, widening in shock.

I panicked, dropping the disguise and activating stealth mode, and charged at Henry. I knocked him onto his back, snatched up my doru, and fled down the hallway, running as fast as my legs could carry me.

[24]

I raced up the spiral staircase to the first administrative level, two floors above the gephyra chamber. Following my link to Meg, I wound my way through the warren of offices and cubicles, pausing just around the corner from the room where I sensed Meg's mind. More familiar minds surrounded her, but I focused instead on the pair of unfamiliar minds belonging to the Order soldiers guarding the door to their prison.

I set down the power core so I could grip the doru with both hands, and then I stepped out from behind the corner and hit each guard with a quick, stunning energy blast. They dropped to the floor, unconscious, and I grabbed the power core and rushed forward.

I burst into the room and found Meg and the others on their feet, waiting for me. Meg stood directly in front of the doorway, crouched and ready to fight. My mom and Emi stood off to Meg's right, one hand each on the childlike Tsakali scout's arms, its wrists still bound together behind its back, but its head and mouth uncovered. Fiona bounced on her heels to Meg's left, her bottom lip caught between her teeth. I scanned the room, peering behind the others, but Raiden and Hades were nowhere to be seen.

"They're not here," Meg said, straightening.

My brow furrowed, and I shook my head.

"Henry took the guys," my mom said, then spat, "the bastard."

My lips parted, my heart beating faster. "Took them *where*?" All of us needed to go—*now*.

Emi shook her head, but it was my mom who spoke. "Henry mentioned an experiment," she said, her tone laden with disgust. "Said it was going to 'change the world'." She used air quotes on the final three words.

"Damn it!" I hissed, my grip tightening on the doru's grooved shaft. Why couldn't it ever be easy? Huffing out a breath, I marched toward Meg and handed her my doru and the power core, then raised my hands to the golden collar encircling her neck.

The collar popped open with a click, and I chucked it across the room. Meg handed the power core and doru back to me, then brought her hands up to her neck, rubbing the exposed skin as gratitude flowed through our bond. I placed my hand on her shoulder in a silent *your welcome* before turning to my mom.

"I'll get you guys through the gephyra," I told her, my focus sliding over to Emi. "And then I'll come back for Raiden and Hades."

There was a ferocious glint in Emi's eyes. "We can help you," she said, her voice razor sharp. Henry had taken her son, after all.

Much as I admired her courage, I shook my head. "You'll only get in my way."

Emi looked stricken.

"Cora!" my mom admonished.

I flashed them both an apologetic smile but didn't take it back. "I'm sorry, Mom, but it's true. Besides, the fewer of you who are here, the less leverage Henry has against me." How many times now had he used my loved ones against me to get what he wanted? Four times? Five? More? I had lost count.

My mom scowled but didn't argue further.

I turned to Fiona and handed her the power core. "Think you can get this thing hooked up in the *Elysium*?" She had been trailing Hades around everywhere he went, soaking up as much knowledge as she could about Olympian tech and how it worked. I just hoped it was enough.

The corner of Fiona's mouth tensed as she studied the power core, adjusting her grip on the heavy device. After a long moment, she nodded.

"Good," I said. "Prep the ship as much as you can. As soon as we join you, we'll power up and take off." I scanned each of their faces, finally settling on Meg's. "Ready?"

She nodded, and I could sense her desire to crack some Order skulls through our bond.

Doru at the ready, I lead the group down the spiral staircase to the gephyra chamber. We paused on the landing outside the cavernous room, ducking out of sight of the Order minions working within. Once again, I was relieved to find the bridge to the frozen settlement still active.

And yet, something felt off. After our encounter down in the mainframe, Henry must have known I would free the others. Why hadn't he sent any of his people after me?

I caught Meg's eye, refocusing on the task at hand. "Can you send a psychic blast into the room that will stun everyone in there?" I wanted to preserve as much of my psychic energy as possible for rescuing Raiden and Hades. There was no predicting what that might involve.

Nodding, Meg closed her eyes. A moment later, she vanished from sight. I could still sense her mind, but I couldn't see her as she moved through the doorway and into the gephyra chamber.

A dull concussion popped my ears, followed by the *thunks* of bodies hitting the floor.

I peeked around the edge of the doorway just in time to see Meg wink back into sight barely a dozen paces into the chamber. She was the only one standing, with at least a dozen unconscious people sprawled all around her.

"All right, let's go," I said, waving the others into the room as I hung back. I couldn't believe we hadn't encountered any Order soldiers yet, but I wasn't willing to count on our luck holding out for much longer. "Hurry!"

Meg led the way to the gephyra, and I guarded the rear. Fiona crossed the bridge first, then my mom with the Tsakali scout, and then Emi. Meg climbed the first step of the platform but paused and turned to face me. I could sense her desire to stay. To help.

I shook my head. "Keep them safe," I said, a plea in my voice. "They mean everything to me. I wouldn't trust anyone else with the job."

Meg stared at me for a long moment, then nodded and turned away from me. In two steps, she was gone.

[25]

I was alone—surrounded by unconscious humans, but alone, nonetheless. Leaning on my doru, I stared at the quicksilver orb marking the opening to the interstellar bridge, wishing we all still had our comms patches, or at least that my bond with Meg could span the lightyears that now separated us.

Sighing, I turned away from the gephyra and jogged over to the control panel near the side of the chamber. I stopped and worried my bottom lip as I scanned the three unconscious people lying on the floor behind the curved desk, considering which to wake. I needed intel—where had Henry taken Raiden and Hades? And what, exactly, was he up to? Figuring the oldest among them was most likely the one in charge, I crouched down beside a man lying on his back with short, salt-and-pepper hair and lined, leathery skin.

I planted one knee on the floor and placed my free hand on the man's forehead, then closed my eyes and concentrated on his dormant mind. I probed psychic fingers into his brain, deeper and deeper until I reached the hypothalamus, then sent out a micro shock to stimulate the region.

I opened my eyes and watched the man's eyelids flutter,

shifting my hand from his forehead to his chest, directly over his heart, before he had fully roused. A moment later, he blinked up at me, and confusion twisted his features.

"I can stop your heart before you can even think about fighting me off," I told him, speaking English rather than his native Arabic, since a quick dip into his mind told me he was fluent in both. "Don't try to sit up. In fact, best not to move at all."

He gulped as fear replaced his confusion. It seeped out of him, flavoring the air.

While he came to grips with the situation, I plucked a few relevant pieces of information about who he was and what he did for the Order from his mind. His name was Kahlil, and he was a physicist—one of the Order's top guys—and he spent most of his time in labs studying alien tech, not out in the field, being attacked by the aliens themselves. He had a wife and three grown children, two of which had children of their own, and he was terrified that he would never get to see them again. Perfect. I could use that fear.

"Here's the deal, Kahlil," I said matter-of-factly. "You tell me what I want to know, and I'll let you live to see your family again. You *don't* tell me what I want to know, and, well . . ." The implication that I would kill him simply for withholding information from me was a lie, but he didn't need to know that. I would simply stun him back to deep unconsciousness, then wake one of his buddies and start the whole process over.

"Wh—what do you want to know?"

I flashed him a razor-sharp grin. "Where is Hades?" I asked. Not that I wanted to find Hades more than I wanted to find Raiden, but I figured it was far more likely that Kahlil, here, would have some idea of where Henry had taken the alien than the human.

"I—I—" Kahlil stuttered, fear paralyzing his tongue. In his mind, I sensed that his fear of Henry and what the maniacal leader of the Order would do to him should he talk was greater than his fear of dying at my hand. I could also sense that he knew where Hades was—where Henry had taken both Hades *and* Raiden.

I bared my teeth at Kahlil. "Where are they?" I demanded. Lucky for me, I didn't need him to actually *tell* me where they had been taken. I just needed him to think about it.

Sweat broke out on Kahlil's forehead, but he remained steadfastly silent.

Narrowing my eyes, I dug a little deeper into his mind and snatched the information I needed. They were in the Genetec tower, next door. There was something about a test or trial of some kind, but Kahlil didn't know the details.

Without another word, I sent a stunning pulse of psychic energy into Kahlil, returning him to unconsciousness, then stood and ran back to the spiral staircase, activating my suit's stealth mode as I went. I raced down to the ground floor, across the lobby, and out through the main doors. Once I was outside, I sprinted across the grounds to the Genetec tower.

Dozens of Order soldiers patrolled around the tower, telling me this was why nobody had hunted me down after I knocked Henry on his ass and fled from the mainframe. They had cut their losses with me and the others and regrouped—here. But *why*?

As I drew closer to the building, I cast out my psychic radar, searching the sea of minds for any familiar mental signatures. I could feel Henry's mind back in the central tower. Was he in the gephyra chamber now, admiring our wreckage? Or perhaps on the fourth floor, confirming that the others had escaped? It didn't really matter, so long as he was elsewhere. Not here.

I focused my psychic radar on the way ahead. As I slipped into the Genetec tower, Raiden's mind pinged my radar, closely followed by Hades' mind. I barreled across the lobby and up the broad, open flight of stairs leading to the second floor. Following the lure of their minds, I slowed to a jog as I made my way down a hallway to the transference lab.

Once upon a time, this lab had housed the Alpha site's most prized tech—the equipment that would have transferred Olympian consciousnesses into human hosts, giving my people a second chance at a natural existence. Poseidon had put an end to that plan the second his god delusions drove him to sabotage the equipment.

I slowed to a walk as I neared the door to the transference lab. This was the most guarded lab in the entire tower and had been equipped with every possible security measure, including a field that would suppress my psychic gifts the instant I stepped into the lab. I could already feel my psychic powers stuttering out here in the hallway.

I stopped at the door, knowing the second I stepped foot in the lab, my powers would be gone, and my doru would be down-graded to a fancy looking fighting staff. I silently berated myself for not commandeering any of the guns I had come across since escaping from my prison cell. Too late now.

While I still had tenuous access to my powers, I inched closer to the door, focusing on the minds within. I wanted to gather as much information about what was happening in there as possible before storming in half-cocked.

I could tell that Raiden was afraid and that Hades was angry. No, he was beyond angry. He was enraged. But with my powers weakened by the anti-psychic field, I couldn't glean much more than their general emotional states. There were two other minds in the lab with them—Order soldiers acting as guards, I assumed —one hovering near Hades, the other near Raiden, their attention focused on their respective charges.

That was it, just the four of them. Nobody on the door. It wasn't a worst-case scenario, which was kind of nice, for once.

Crouching low, I reached into the door panel with psychic fingers and slid the door open as slowly and quietly as possible.

Hades, Raiden, and their guards were on a raised, circular dais in the center of the lab. Dozens of workstations encircled the dais in three consecutive rings, steel desks with stacks of drawers tucked beneath and topped with sleek Olympian equipment, providing me some cover. Once the door panel was open just enough for me to squeeze through, I crept into the lab and manually eased the door shut again.

Quickly, silently, I crawled to the nearest workstation and huddled behind a set of drawers, then peeked around the desk to scan the situation. Hades was perched on a stool in front of a curved desk trimmed with golden orichalcum, a holoscreen hovering in front of him. Based on the desk's extravagant appearance, I figured it was the control panel for the transference equipment.

Hades' attention wasn't on the holoscreen, but lower, on the tech built into the desk. He held a small tool of some kind in one hand and sat hunched over the surface, focused on the inner workings of the control panel. An Order soldier stood behind him, his assault rifle trained on Hades' back.

I ducked behind the workstation once more and focused on taking slow, even breaths. I needed to keep calm, to act, not react. One wrong move, and Hades could be riddled with bullet holes.

After one last long, slow deep breath, I peeked around the other side of the workstation and studied Raiden on the opposite side of the dais. He was gagged and sitting in something that looked an awful lot like a high-tech electric chair, his arms, shoulders, and head held immobile by steel restraints. My view of the lower half of his body was blocked by another workstation, but I assumed the rest of him was similarly restrained. And like Hades, Raiden was being held at gunpoint.

The sight made my blood boil, and I gritted my teeth, ducking back behind the workstation. I could move from workstation to workstation until I was close enough to incapacitate

Raiden's guard, then use his weapon to take out the guard on Hades, if Hades wasn't able to overwhelm the guard himself. It was far from a sure thing. It would either work, or some or all of us would die. But I had to try.

Before I could scuttle to the next workstation, the door panel to the hallway slid open, and Henry strode into the lab, flanked by six more Order soldiers. He stopped two steps into the lab and let his guards glide in past him.

All six immediately trained their weapons on me.

[26]

"We must stop meeting this way, ancient one," Henry said, clasping his hand behind his back, clearly pleased by discovering me here.

I mentally kicked myself for not snapping his stupid neck when I'd tackled him down in the mainframe.

"I see that you are once again drained of your powers." He scanned the lab. "I had not realized this place was warded against your kind." Menace danced in his eyes when he smiled. "It would seem even your own people did not trust you." He approached slowly, letting his guards adjust around him. "Stand up, ancient one, and keep your hands where we can see them." He stopped several paces away, his stare flicking to my doru. "Leave the weapon on the floor."

I held the doru out in front of me and glared up at him as I started to stand.

"Ah ah," Henry said, waving his finger at me like I was a misbehaving child. "Place the weapon on the floor and roll it to me, *then* stand."

I hesitated before setting the doru on the floor. I pushed it toward him with minimal effort and maximum irritation. The doru stopped rolling halfway there, out of my reach, but also out of his. If he wanted it, he would have to get a little bit closer to me. Too close for comfort.

"Oops," I said as I stood up the rest of the way, my glare locking with Henry's. "My bad."

A muscle twitched in his cheek. "Turn around," he ordered.

I did as instructed, my eyes meeting first Raiden's concerned stare, then Hades'.

"Very good," Henry said from behind me. "Let us all understand the situation and see that there is no more hope for escape. It is better this way—to know, to accept our fate."

My mind whirled as I tried to pull some comprehensible meaning from Henry's cryptic words. What *fate* was he talking about? What, exactly, was he planning?

The sole of his shoe squeaked on the polished tile floor as he stepped closer to me, likely to retrieve my doru. Maybe if I had still been facing him, I could have lunged and taken him hostage before his guards got trigger happy, but I didn't like my odds when I was blind to what was happening behind me. Odds were, it wasn't even Henry at all, but one of his lackeys picking up the staff for him.

"Walk up to the dais and kneel on the floor," Henry commanded. "Bear witness to my great accomplishment."

The scathing look Hades sent Henry told me all I needed to know about what the Olympian thought of Henry and his *great accomplishment*. No doubt, Hades was the true owner of this *great accomplishment*, his hard work boosting Henry's ego. Clearly it had to do with the transference equipment Hades was repairing. He must have found all the necessary parts during our explorations of the lost colonies.

But what I couldn't figure out was Raiden's role in all of this. I'd had enough encounters with Henry to know he had a penchant for the tell-all variety of gloating villainous monologues. I held out hope that his nature would hold true, though I figured it wouldn't hurt to give him a little nudge.

I approached the circular dais at the center of the lab, my steps slow as I played through all my available next moves. With so many guns aimed not just at me but also at Raiden and Hades, I was very aware that I needed to proceed with extreme caution.

"It looks to me like Hades is doing all the work," I tossed over my shoulder as I climbed the five shallow steps up to the dais. "What exactly is *your* accomplishment here?" I knelt, keeping my back to Henry, hoping my inattention to him prodded him further, and watched Raiden. His focus was past me, on Henry, and I waited for any sign or indication that my goading was working. So far, the primicerius was showing remarkable restraint.

Slow footsteps behind me that I assumed belonged to Henry marked his progress as he trailed me, but once again, he stopped outside of easy striking distance.

At present, the only move I could see was to lure him close enough that I could take him hostage and hold his life as collateral for our freedom.

"It must make you feel big and powerful to order around someone like Hades," I said, then fell quiet, letting the implied meaning sink in—that Hades was better than Henry. All you needed was a set of working eyeballs to see that, but Henry struck me as the delusions-of-grandeur type.

"Have you ever watched a grandmaster play chess?" Henry asked me, close enough behind me to confirm that he had been the one following me after all. Perfect.

I suppressed a smile.

"They play so far ahead that by the second move," he went on, "they can already see the end of the game."

I rolled my eyes. He definitely suffered from delusions of grandeur.

"The leaders of this world lack the spark of creativity required for such foresight," Henry continued.

I narrowed my eyes, thinking my prodding may have worked. Villainous monologue, here we come.

"And so," Henry said, "I will replace them."

My focus snapped from Raiden to Hades as I processed this new information. Hades was repairing a machine that could transfer a consciousness into a new host body. That much was obvious. Henry wanted to replace the world leaders, which clearly required the transference equipment. But whose consciousnesses was he planning on using to overwrite the world leaders' minds? Order members? Duplicates of his own consciousness? Or . . .

My eyes opened wider as realization dawned.

Was Henry attempting to overwrite the minds of the world's leaders with Olympians?

Shock parted my lips, and I searched Hades' expression for confirmation of my suspicion. He glanced my way, just for a moment, and nodded minutely.

I couldn't believe it. Henry was really going to do it. And he was *crazy enough* to do it.

The part of me that was still scarred by the ancient betrayals that had ended my previous life wondered if Hades was participating willingly, knowing this would revive some of our people, at least in spirit. But then my focus shifted to the guard standing behind him, holding him at gunpoint, and the part of me that loved him knocked all such thoughts away. Hades was not a willing accomplice.

My attention returned to Raiden, restrained in that terrifying chair contraption. I still couldn't puzzle out his role in all of this. Henry would have had a reason for bringing Raiden here—he was too much trouble, otherwise. As I studied the tech-heavy chair Raiden was tied to, a terrible fear seeped into my bones, chilling me from the inside out.

I had never been in this lab before, and I didn't know anything about how the transference equipment worked, other than that during the transference process, a consciousness was pulled from storage—either those in short-term storage here in the Alpha site or those in long-term storage at the Omega site. From what I understood, the great transference Poseidon had originally planned before being driven mad by the prospect of immortality—or rather, *losing* the relative immortality granted to him by cloning—involved a massive remote transference targeting all humans in a specified geographic location.

But, I knew a consciousness could also be transferred through a direct connection, which was how my own consciousness had been transferred from my old body to my new clone each cycle, as with every other Olympian who had lived on this planet. But the transfer had always happened when we were infants, before our neural structure had had a chance to solidify into any permanent, identity-forming patterns.

I narrowed my eyes, staring through Raiden, as I mentally fit all the puzzle pieces together. The Olympian scientists who had developed the equipment for the great transference would have needed a way to experiment on adult human subjects with fully formed brains, as those were to be the new hosts to the Olympian consciousnesses. Was that what this chair was for—testing the efficacy of the transference equipment on live, adult subjects? The same chair that Raiden was currently sitting in?

Rage turned my heart into a sledgehammer trying to slam through my sternum. Clenching my jaw, I looked over my shoulder at Henry, who stood maybe five paces back. "Why is Raiden here?"

Henry's thin lips spread into a slow grin. "From your expression, I think you've already figured that out." His pale eyes sparkled with malicious glee. "How wonderful it is that you will be here to witness the first transfer—the rebirth of your people."

His smile faded, his expression darkening. "You should thank me for letting you stay."

I was doused in a wash of icy hatred. "If you hurt him, I will kill you," I promised. "Slowly and with great pleasure."

Again, that muscle in Henry's cheek twitched. "I have no doubt," he murmured. "But I have no intention of hurting Raiden. Rather, I wish to elevate him. To *enlighten* him."

"You're going to destroy everything that makes him, *him*," I spat, glaring. "It's murder."

My glare snapped to Hades. "I can't believe you're helping him." I shook my head and made a disgusted sound low in my throat.

Hades glanced up from the guts of the control panel to look at me.

My focus shifted to the guard behind him, then back to Hades. Held at gunpoint or not, there was no excuse for going along with this.

Hades' stare slipped away from mine as he returned to his work.

"You could have said no," I blurted, my voice raw and tears stinging my eyes. "You could have saved him. This is the only lifetime he gets, but you've had, what—twenty, thirty cycles? It isn't enough? You still need more?" My chest heaved with each breath as my fear and rage swept all rationality away.

Hades went very still. "I'm not doing this to save myself," he said, his voice perfectly even and razor sharp. "I'm doing it to save you." His eyes met mine. "It would seem you are more trouble than you're worth. You were to be executed." He glanced down at the control panel, his eyebrows raised. "I made sure that didn't happen."

"You traded Raiden's life for mine," I said, my voice hollow. I felt ill, like the place where my stomach should have been was now a rotting, festering lump. This was my fault. Raiden's predicament—his impending doom—was because of me. Because Hades loved me.

Hades stood a little straighter, holding his head high. "I did what needed to be done to ensure you survived," he said, his voice steady, his stare unwavering. "I was looking out for your best interests, as always."

My heart lodged in my throat, and I wanted to cry. To scream. To rage at Hades that he had chosen wrong. I wasn't worth this. I wasn't worth Raiden's life.

Desperate for something to tether me to reality, to keep the rage and fear and sorrow from tearing me apart, I looked at Raiden. At strong, sweet, stoic Raiden. At the gentle man who had survived one level of hell only to be dumped back into another.

And as my eyes met his, his resigned expression shattered my heart.

[27]

As I stared at Raiden, I saw flashes of our childhood together. Of combing the beach near Blackthorn Manor in search of hermit crabs and pretty shells. Of hanging out in the fort we had built in the woods. Of staying up late lying on our backs on a blanket on the lawn near the edge of the bluff, staring up at the stars and imagining what else might be out there. Of watching him leave for boot camp and wondering if he would ever return.

And throughout all those memories, a single thought spun around and around in my head: it's not fair. Hades had lived dozens of lifetimes, and I had lived more than my fair share. But Raiden only had the one lifetime. This lifetime.

Bowing my head, I silently vowed that Raiden's single shot at life wouldn't be cut short. Not here. Not today. Not while there was still breath in my lungs and blood in my veins.

Fueled by the desperate conviction to save the one person in this lab who deserved to live, I dove across the dais, sliding around the transference chair on my side, my arms outstretched ahead of me. Deafening gunfire filled the lab.

"Hold your fire!" Henry shouted.

I snagged the left ankle of Raiden's guard and yanked his

legs out from underneath him before he could react. Without a second thought, I snapped his neck, embracing the irony of taking one human life in order to save another. In the sudden silence, the soldier's body hit the floor with a resounding *thump*.

I had never been afraid to admit that some lives mattered to me more than others. It was part of being self-aware, of knowing all life eventually came to an end. To some, it was their own life that mattered most. To others, it was the lives of the people they loved. To me, in this moment, it was Raiden's.

I relieved the dead soldier of his assault rifle and armed myself, then rolled off the dais and ducked behind one of the many workstations encircling the platform. I peeked over the top of the desk, scanning the lab with the barrel of my new gun.

I half expected Hades to use the distraction to fight off his own guard, especially knowing that Henry wouldn't risk the Olympian's life until his machine was finished, and he had proof that it worked. Proof in the form of some random Olympian walking around wearing Raiden's body like its favorite suit. But Hades just stood there, watching the chaos unfold, doing nothing.

Henry, on the other hand, had ducked out of sight while I was taking out Raiden's guard, and I figured he was hiding behind another of the workstations. His cease-fire order told me he wanted the transference equipment intact more than he wanted me dead. Good to know. I could work with that.

A head poked around the side of a workstation across the room, and I didn't hesitate to shift my aim and pull the trigger. Another Order soldier's body hit the floor. I picked off another in the same way, and for the gazillionth time in the last month, I felt like I had fallen into one of the video games I loved so much, picking off bad guys in an epic showdown. That strange sensation helped to dull the reality that I was ending the lives of real people.

I ducked back behind the workstation and prepared to move

to another hiding spot. I huddled at the edge of the workstation, gathering my strength and coiling my muscles.

"Come out, come out, ancient one," Henry taunted. From the sound of his voice, I had the impression he was on the dais now. With Hades and Raiden.

Heart sinking into my stomach, I peeked around the side of the desk.

Henry stood beside Raiden, using the larger man's body and the chair to block any potential shot I had at him. He held a pistol in his hand, the muzzle of the gun pressed against Raiden's temple.

"Shit," I hissed and pulled back behind the workstation.

Breathing hard, I weighed my options. I could chance a shot. I might be able to hit Henry and miss Raiden. But if I missed, all Henry needed to do was pull the trigger, and Raiden would be dead. Or I could surrender and let Henry have his way. At least Raiden's body would live on, even if the soul within belonged to another. I gritted my teeth, hating that option.

"He is too much of a liability," Henry said, his sing-song accent like nails on a chalkboard to my ears. "He knows too much about the Order . . . too much about your kind. He can either live on as an Olympian, or he can die as himself." Henry fell quiet for a moment, letting his words sink in. "Many of my people would be honored to take his place, so his death would be no great loss to me."

I squeezed my eyes shut and pounded my fist against my leg.

"The choice is yours, ancient one," Henry announced. "You can decide his fate, right here, right now. Life as an Olympian, or death as a human—what will it be?"

Feeling trapped, I peered over the top of the workstation to reassess the situation. Hades at the control panel, his guard behind him. Four more Order soldiers hidden throughout the lab. Raiden in the transference chair. Henry behind him. Me, crouched here, useless.

There was nothing I could do. No way out of this that I could see. I had to choose.

Slowly, I stood, aiming my rifle in Henry's direction. My eyes locked with Raiden's as I struggled with the impossible choice. I wanted to apologize to him, to tell him how sorry I was for turning his world upside down, then tearing it apart. But the words withered and died in my throat.

I had failed him. I was failing him right now. There was nothing I could do to save him. I wasn't good enough. And now, one way or another, he was going to die.

"How much longer, Hades?" Henry snapped. "My patience is not endless . . ."

I looked at Hades, pleading with my eyes for him to say he needed more time.

His eyes met mine for the briefest moment before his attention shifted to Henry. "It's ready now."

I hunched over as if I had been physically gutted by his words. By his betrayal. He could have pretended it wasn't ready yet. He could have bought me some more time. Bought Raiden some more time. But maybe he didn't want that. Maybe he saw this as a way to eliminate the final obstacle to my heart. To finally claim his prize.

My stare narrowed to a glare. I would kill him. Henry first, then Hades. It would hurt, ending his life, but I would do it. This was the last time he would ever betray me.

Hades' focus shifted back to me. His expression was calm, not the least bit repentant, no hint of apology. His complete disregard slashed through my anger and eroded my certainty. His reaction felt off, and once again, I reassessed the situation.

Was I wrong about Hades? I truly hoped I was.

He was no idiot—quite the opposite in fact—and the more I thought about it, the less I believed he would risk losing me over a petty rivalry. A rivalry he hardly felt, no less. Monogamy wasn't a thing in Olympian society, and Hades *didn't* view

Raiden as an obstacle standing between us. That was me—the Cora part of me—projecting my American values on him. The only obstacle standing between Hades and me was *me*. And the only sure way to ensure he would lose me forever would be to willfully eliminate Raiden as a candidate for my heart.

Which meant there was only one reason he *wouldn't* delay the transference for as long as possible—only one reason he *wouldn't* buy me time to find another way out of this. He already had a plan.

Hades' steady gaze and calm demeanor took on a new meaning, and I felt as certain as I could be without actually being able to read his mind that he was telling me—asking me—to trust him. My gut told me to trust him, too.

I held Hades' stare for a moment longer, then closed my eyes, silently hoping that my trust in Hades wasn't misplaced. That he was offering me a third choice—a blind choice, but a better choice.

Inhaling deeply, I opened my eyes and looked at Henry. "Start the transference."

[28]

I leaned my hip against the edge of the workstation, my arms crossed over my chest and the rifle discarded on the desk, and watched Hades reassemble the cover of the control panel. The guard behind Hades had relaxed, his rifle now aimed at the floor. Henry, too, had lowered his weapon and held the handgun alongside his thigh as he paced back and forth across the dais. The four other Order soldiers stood around the perimeter of the lab, far from me, their assault rifles trained on Raiden, to ensure I behaved.

Hades snapped one last part back in place, then looked up, his eyes meeting mine. "It's ready," he said softly, almost like he was trying for a somber tone. But the glint in his eyes hinted at barely contained excitement.

Henry stopped pacing, looking back and forth from Hades to me. I could practically feel his irritation at Hades for looking to me rather than to him for the final go-ahead.

I stared at Hades for a long moment, then nodded.

"Initiate the transference," Henry said, his order redundant after my nod.

Hades glanced at Henry dismissively, then turned his attention to the holoscreen hovering in front of him and started adjusting dials and flipping switches on the control panel.

Raiden's stare was boring a hole in my cheek, and I forced myself to look at him. To see the desperation in his eyes. It was an effort to school my features. To keep my expression blank. I wanted nothing more than to reassure him that everything was going to be all right—even though I didn't know what exactly was going to happen once the transference began. Within me, my trust in Hades warred with my fear for Raiden, and doubt seeped in. What if I was wrong?

As the machine powered up, the floor of the dais started to glow with a soft azure light, and a low hum filled the lab. I held my breath, waiting for a flash or a bang or *something* to happen that would let me in on Hades' plan. But nothing more seemed to be happening beyond that gentle glow and low hum. My only comfort was that Raiden appeared completely unaffected. His survival was all that mattered to me at the moment.

Henry stalked over to the control panel to lurk beside Hades, like he wanted to make sure Hades didn't do something to sabotage the transference, despite having no understanding of how the machine worked. "Why isn't anything happening to him?" Henry asked, his voice demanding. "Is it supposed to take this long?"

Hades didn't even glance at the other man. He simply continued to tweak the controls and monitor the readings on the holoscreen. "I am attempting to overwrite a human mind with a foreign consciousness," he explained, a hint of condescension seeping into his tone. "There are many steps involved. It is not an instantaneous sprocess." This answer only seemed to irritate Henry, rubbing his nose in his own ignorance in the process.

"If this doesn't work . . . ." As Henry's words trailed off, his glare drifted my way, the implied threat loud and clear. If Hades screwed up—accidentally or on purpose—then I was dead. Henry's control over the situation was slipping, and all his blustering and looming was his way of attempting to reclaim the reins.

I fought the urge to roll my eyes and returned my attention to Raiden, searching his features for some sign of pain or discomfort. But all I could see was the desperation in his eyes. The fear that this was it for him.

"I have already extracted the consciousness from storage and am spooling it within the transference matrix," Hades explained, annoyance edging into his voice. "Soon, the host will be sedated, and the overwriting process will begin."

"How long will it take?" Henry asked.

I glanced at the pair at the control panel. Hades' attention was still focused on what he was doing, but Henry was staring at Raiden, a hungry gleam in his eyes.

"There is no standard time range," Hades told him. "It depends on the neural structure of the host's mind. It could take minutes. It could take hours." He pulled his hands from the controls, and I had the sense that he was waiting for something.

Silence filled the lab, bringing with it a thick cloud of tension that set me even more on edge. A musical trio of *dings* shattered the silence, and I jumped.

"The Olympian consciousness is spooled and primed," Hades informed us, then pushed a button on the control panel. "Initiating the sedation process."

I returned my attention to Raiden and watched his eyelids droop as his features slackened. My heart beat faster, and I wrapped my arms around my middle, my fingers digging into my sides. Once again, doubt seeped in, and I second-guessed my decision to trust Hades with Raiden's life. I stared at Raiden, hard, looking for some sign that he was faking the sudden drowsiness, that it was all an act.

Soon, Raiden was slumped against his restraints, unconscious, so far as I could tell.

I swallowed hard, barely managing to suppress the panic attempting to claw its way out of me.

Motion in my peripheral vision caught my eye, and I tore my stare from Raiden to see one of the Order soldiers stationed near the wall let go of his rifle and raise his hands to clutch either side of his head. He groaned in pain.

Another joined him, then the other two, until all four of the Order soldiers posted around the periphery of the lab were clutching their heads and filling the room with their groans.

I straightened, no longer leaning against the edge of the desk, and lowered my arms.

"What's happening?" Henry asked, his hard voice cutting through the chorus of groans. He looked from guard to guard, his confusion quickly replaced by suspicion as he turned to Hades. "What are you doing to them?"

Hades remained calm in the face of the smaller man's accusations, only the slightest frown turning down the corners of his mouth and the faintest line appearing between his brows. "I believe the resonance of the transference equipment may be causing them some mild neural discomfort," he offered, unconcerned. "It should pass momentarily."

I inched over to the next workstation, slowly making my way closer to Raiden.

One of the Order soldiers near the edge of the lab dropped to his knees. Henry raised his gun arm and aimed his handgun at Hades' head, but quickly shifted his aim to me.

I froze, my stare locking with Henry's.

There was panic in his eyes, and possibly the hint of pain.

The soldier behind Henry and Hades raised his hands, gripping the sides of his head, his groans joining the others.

Eyes wild, Henry glanced at the guard, but quickly returned his attention to Hades and me. "You're doing this on purpose," he accused shrilly, shaking his gun in my direction. "Make it stop, or I will kill her!"

Hades turned to Henry as the other man's gun arm inched lower. "No," Hades said, "you will do no such thing."

Henry hunched in on himself, clutching either side of his head, the pistol still in hand.

All the Order soldiers were on the floor now. Two were on their knees, two were lying on their sides, writhing in pain, and one lay completely still.

"In fact," Hades continued, "you will never threaten her again."

Cautiously, I rounded the workstation and approached the dais. Raiden was still slumped in his restraints, unconscious. "What's happening?" I asked Hades as I ascended the steps.

The pistol slipped from Henry's grasp, and he dropped to his knees, letting out an agonized groan. His body seemed to go boneless, and he flopped onto his side on the floor, where he writhed and twitched.

"He is being overwritten," Hades said, watching the fallen human with unveiled disgust. Hades waited until he fell still, then looked at me. "They all are."

[29]

I rushed across the dais to Raiden and pulled the gag out of his mouth before tugging on his steel bindings. He still sat slumped in the chair, clearly unconscious. But at least it was a sedative that had knocked him out, and not his mind being overwritten, like Henry and his soldiers.

"Don't free him yet," Hades said from his position at the control panel behind me. "It's not safe."

I stopped tugging on the steel cuff securing Raiden's wrist to the arm of the chair and glanced back at Hades.

"We must wait until the overwriting process is complete," he said. Every few seconds, he adjusted this or that dial, his eyes glued to the holoscreen as he continued to direct the transference process.

I straightened, giving up on manually freeing Raiden, and turned around, planting my hands on my hips. "What do you mean?"

"I set the machine to remote transference mode, targeting all human minds within a one-mile radius," Hades explained, only glancing at me briefly. "Raiden is hooked up for a direct transference, and his placement in that exact location"—Hades sent a pointed look past me at the transference chair and its lone occupant—"is the only thing protecting him from being overwritten, as well."

I chewed on my bottom lip and studied Raiden, seeing his restraints in a whole new light. Strangely, they were protecting him.

"If you move him," Hades continued, "he will be targeted by the system, and there will be nothing I can do to stop it. As a failsafe to protect any Olympian consciousness spooled in the matrix, there is no way to shut off the machine. To do so would destroy any Olympian currently floating in limbo." Hades shook his head. "We have no choice but to let it run its course."

I scanned the limp forms of the Order soldiers scattered around the lab. It was crazy to think that soon, they wouldn't be Order soldiers. They would be Olympians, in mind if not in body. "How long will it take?"

"The overwriting process should be complete within five minutes or so," Hades said, adjusting another dial on the control panel. "The consciousnesses will then need to settle into their new host brains. They should wake about an hour after the transference is complete."

After one last glance at Raiden, I made my way over to the control panel to join Hades. I stopped at the edge of the desk and stared down at my former nemesis. The next time he opened his eyes, he would be someone else entirely. Henry Magnusson was gone.

"Who are they?" I asked. "Or, I guess, who *will they be*?"

Hades stared at the holoscreen for a moment, then flipped a switch on the control panel. There was a note of finality to the motion. Exhaling heavily, he raised his hands to scrub his face and combed his fingers through his hair, smoothing it down over his skull. He looked utterly exhausted.

"My team," he finally said in answer to my question about the newly transferred Olympian identities. "People I trust, and people with the technical know-how to help us navigate the coming crisis."

I nodded to myself, thinking that made sense. Hades' team was filled with the best and brightest scientists our species had to offer. They had been in charge of all cloning and genetic enhancements in the Alpha site, including the process that transformed regular female Olympians into psychically-enabled Amazon warriors, not to mention the subtle genetic guidance we had provided humanity during our centuries as hidden custodians of this planet. Then there was the development of the transference equipment, too. If anyone could come up with a way of defending this planet and defeating the Tsakali—or, more likely, setting up a new human-Olympian settlement on some far-off planet when we fled from Earth—it was Hades' team.

"They'll be confused when they wake," Hades said. "They'll need immediate guidance . . . someone to help them transition into their new existence."

My eyes locked with his. "Why do I get the impression that you're going to ask me to babysit them?" I tilted my head to the side and pursed my lips. "You're the one who woke them up. You're their leader. Don't you think you should be here to greet them?" My focus drifted back down to Henry's body. How was I going to look past the monster he had been to see the Olympian he had become?

Hades frowned and raised his holoband, pulling up the screen. The crease between his brows deepened with worry. "I wish I could stay and welcome them into this new life, but the Omega site is nearing critical failure. I must return and install a new power core as soon as possible. I could wait until they wake, but . . ." Hades raised one shoulder. "The longer I wait, the greater the risk of critical failure."

I sighed. "I sent the new power core through the gephyra with the others," I admitted reluctantly, then flashed Hades an apologetic smile. "Hopefully, Raiden knows what Henry did with the one we found off-world." I hadn't seen it in the gephyra chamber, but then again, I'd kind of forgotten about it and hadn't actually looked for it.

"I saw him pack it into a crate for transport," Hades said, pointing down at Henry's body with his chin. "When he marched us through the gephyra chamber on our way here, the crate was still there. With everything going on, I can't imagine it's been moved since then."

I nodded, relieved that we might have struck a patch of luck, for once. "Fine. You go. Save our people. Again." I smirked, my mood lightening by the second. "I'll stay here to clean up your mess." My eyes met his. "Again."

Hades' lips twisted into a smirk that mirrored mine, and I felt that old, familiar zing of charged tension arc between us. I stepped closer to him, my movements slow and deliberate, until I was very much invading his personal space. I tilted my head back and reached for his hand, linking our fingers together. "Thank you—for saving my life," I told him, then glanced over my shoulder at Raiden, just for a moment. "And for saving his."

Hades raised his free hand to skim his knuckles down my cheek and along my jawline.

I leaned into the caress.

"I know how much he means to you," Hades murmured, his eyes searching mine. "Hurting him hurts you. I would never willingly let anything happen to him."

How could I have doubted him? "But do you know how much *you* mean to me?" I said softly, wetting my lips.

Hades leaned in, his ice-blue eyes glittering with desire. "Why don't you tell me?"

The humming filling the lab faded suddenly; the transference machine was powering down. Hades stopped short of his lips touching mine and shot a sideways glance to the holoscreen, then pulled back. "It's done."

I blinked, startled by the abrupt shift from pleasure to business, and took a step back.

Hades pressed a button on the control panel and looked past me to Raiden. "I've initiated the arousal sequence. He'll wake soon. I can release his restraints now if you wish, but you may want to be there to ensure he doesn't fall forward out of the chair."

A slow smile curved my lips. I was overwhelmed with love for this man, who had gone out of his way to save the only other man on this planet who might keep me from him. He had saved Raiden because I loved *him*, too. If that wasn't pure, selfless love, then such a thing didn't exist.

I stepped closer to Hades and rose on my toes to brush a soft kiss against his lips. "Thank you," I whispered as I pulled away, my eyes locking with his. I wanted him to see how much I appreciated him.

Hades' lips curved into a small smile, and he bowed his head. "For you, anything."

Heart thrumming with happiness, I gave his hand a squeeze, and then I turned and hurried over to Raiden and waited for Hades to release the restraints on the chair.

With a *snick*, the steel bands unlocked, then retracted into the chair. Raiden slumped forward, and I rested a hand on his shoulder to hold him in place. I waited to let go until his muscles stiffened under my hand and his body was no longer limp.

Raiden's eyelids fluttered open, and it took his eyes a moment to really focus on me. "Cora?" he breathed. "What happened?"

"It's over. We won," I said, grinning. "Welcome back."

[30]

The hushed voices of the newly awakened Olympians sitting in clusters on the floor under the grand, arched ceiling of the central tower's lobby echoed as Raiden and I moved from group to group, handing out the meal bars we had pilfered from the Order's supplies. It boggled my mind that hours ago, these people—or, rather, their bodies—had been my enemies, but now they were my people. They were Olympians, in mind, if not in body.

They knew how they had come to be here and who had brought them back, and now they awaited Hades' return from the Omega site, as did I. Thankfully it was night in Egypt, meaning Hades was able to get the *Argo* into the Omega site without being noticed. According to his last check-in, he had finished the repairs, and the Omega sites' mainframe was stable for the first time in millennia. His work there was done, and now it was only a matter of waiting for him to return.

I spotted the body that had been Henry Magnusson, the Primicerius of the Custodes Veritatis and all-around douchebag, in a nearby cluster of Olympians as I approached their group to hand out meal bars to them. His body now housed an Olympian geneticist named Niall, but I couldn't help but wonder if some slivers of Henry's toxic soul was still embedded deep within him. Niall must have sensed me watching him because he looked up. When his eyes met mine, I forced a closed-mouth smile and handed him a meal bar.

Could they reach any of their host's memories, or were the bodies little more than a shell? Having recently been two people in a single body, it was hard not to project my dual-consciousness experience onto them. I felt torn about what had happened to the humans—to the minds that had been overwritten, all but erased from existence. They had chosen this path, given their lives to the Order, and followed Henry to this point. To this end.

But my mom had been one of them once, as had Emi, and from their experience as Order devotees, I knew it wasn't the kind of organization one had the option to walk away from. To join the Order was to sign one's life over. There was no retiring. No chance for a career change. Belonging to the Order was a life commitment—or a life sentence.

Just because these people had come here under Henry's tyrannical command didn't mean they had chosen this particular battle. They hadn't come here of their own free will, and that bothered me more than I would have liked to admit. I had been just like them, once, a brainwashed pawn blindly following Demeter's commands.

An approaching energy signature tripped my psychic radar, far off in the distance, but closing in fast. I hurriedly handed out the remainder of the meal bars before rushing to the doors at the front of the lobby and pushing out into the filtered sunlight seeping in through the thick layer of ice sheltering the city. I watched the *Argo* coast through the hole it had bored into the glacier and glide lower, weaving around the towering buildings.

The small ship landed nearby, and I jogged out to meet Hades as the loading ramp lowered to the ground. Hades appeared, descending the ramp, and I slowed to a walk.

"Glad you're back," I said, reaching out to grip his arm when I reached him.

He stared down at me, his ice-blue eyes filled with warmth. "Glad to be back." The corner of his mouth ticked upward, and the silence stretched out between us, turning expectant.

I cleared my throat and released his arm. "They're, um, all waiting for you in the lobby," I told him, pointing over my shoulder with my thumb.

Hades nodded. "Good. I'm eager to speak with them."

I turned and started back to the central tower, Hades falling in step beside me. Raiden stood in the doorway ahead, holding the door open as he waited for us. Something had shifted between Raiden and Hades. I couldn't put my finger on it, but there was more respect between them now, as though they were both able to fully grasp what the other meant to me. I wasn't sure what it would mean for us moving forward, but I was hopeful that the big, scary either-or I had been dreading wasn't quite so hard and fast.

"Raiden and I are packed and ready to go through the gephyra," I told Hades as we drew near Raiden and the open door. "Do you want us to wait for you, or . . .?"

Hades shook his head. "You should go. Make sure the *Elysium* is prepped. I'll brief our people on the situation and give them guidance on what to work on while they await our return."

I glanced at him sidelong. "And you'll make sure they understand why they need to stay down here . . . no matter what?" I said. "I already told them as much, but I'm sure it will mean more coming from you."

Hades nodded once. "And Tammy should be here," he said, a soft smile curving his lips and warm fondness in his voice. "She'll keep everyone in line." He spoke of his long-time Genetec second-in-command, Tammyris, who had been placed into the body of an unassuming middle-aged woman. The body was perfect, emulating everything I remembered about

Tammyris. She was easy to overlook, but one glimpse into her eyes, and there was no mistaking her keen intelligence or iron will.

Raiden stepped out of the way as Hades and I passed through the doorway into the lobby. Transplanted Olympians rose to their feet all around us.

I stopped and turned to Hades. "Don't take too long. The sooner we can get the *Elysium* off the ground, the sooner we'll get back here to load up the rest of our people." And hopefully, do something to avert the approaching shitstorm that didn't involve nuking this whole planet, I thought but didn't voice.

Now that we had "Henry" on our side, there was a chance we could sway the UN Security Council to our way of thinking. The Tsakali were a plague on the universe, and if the world leaders couldn't see that, there wasn't anything we could do to save this planet.

Hades nodded, his lips curving into an all-business smile. "As you say." He looked at Raiden, and the two men exchanged a nod.

Raiden started for the stairs at the back of the lobby that would carry us up to the gephyra chamber.

I turned to follow but hesitated. Keenly aware of the Olympian eyes watching us, I kept my hands to myself and touched the comms patch stuck behind my ear, meeting Hades' watchful gaze. These people were researchers and scientists, not fighters. I hated leaving them here to fend for themselves. "If you catch even the slightest whiff of trouble . . . ." I raised my eyebrows to emphasize my implied directive.

Hades smiled, warmth in his expression this time. "You'll be the first to know."

I held his stare for a long moment, not liking the idea of splitting up again. But it had to be done. I nodded and turned away, jogging to catch up with Raiden. We hurried up the spiral staircase and into the gephyra chamber, where the quicksilver orb marking the opening of the bridge to the frozen settlement shimmered on the golden platform.

We made a beeline for our packs and weapons propped up against the back of the control panel. Once we were geared up and ready to go, we headed for the gephyra in the center of the room.

"You ready for the next adventure?" Raiden asked as we closed in on the opening to the bridge.

With him by my side, how could I not be? I grinned, shooting him a sideways glance. "Wouldn't miss it for the world."

[31]

Hades and I stood side by side on the balcony overlooking the command center of the *Elysium*, the gephyra dormant behind us while the command stations spread out below us blinked and beeped with activity. The passing stars and other celestial bodies were visible on the massive viewscreen ahead, looking like multi-hued laser beams all converging on some distant point.

I stood facing the viewscreen, gripping the handrail with both hands, my regulator activated to give the others aboard the ship their privacy. Hades stood with his back to the screen, his arms crossed over his chest. My mom sat at the navigation terminal below, while Raiden and Meg were in one of the ship's many training rooms, sparring. Emi and Fiona were huddled together in the lab where the Tsakali scout was being held captive, studying the strange creature.

I hadn't traveled aboard a ship moving at faster-than-light speeds since the *Tartarus* arrived on Earth some fourteen thousand years ago. I had lived at least a dozen lifetimes since, but the lurch of the ship as the FTL engines fired spurred emotions in me that felt a lot like the nostalgia of coming home after having been gone too long.

I had been born aboard the *Tartarus*—or rather, *created*—and my first lifetime had been lived in that relative captivity. Back then, slipping into and out of faster-than-light travel had been a regular and predictable part of my day, like the rising and setting of the sun. It was a strange comfort to once again be contained within a cage of orichalcum-reinforced steel, hurtling across the universe. I wondered if this was what it was like for seafarers when they returned to their beloved ships, to their beloved ocean, after too long on land. Only my ocean was not composed of salt and water, but of space dust and stars.

I glanced at Hades, studying the slight furrow between his eyebrows. He was deep in thought, his stare locked on the gephyra's golden platform, though I had the impression he wasn't really looking at the machine so much as using it as a focal point for his wandering thoughts.

"Do you ever miss it?" I asked him.

Blinking, Hades looked at me, confusion clouding his stare.

I gestured to the viewscreen behind him, a small, dreamy smile touching my lips. "Soaring among the stars . . ."

Hades glanced over his shoulder, raising his eyebrows. "Not really, no," he said and returned to staring ahead. After a moment, his attention slid back to me. "You miss it?"

I shrugged. "For a long time, it was all I knew," I reminded him.

Unlike almost all other engineered Olympians created during the multi-cycle trip from Olympus to Earth, my eyes had been opened to the truth of our existence early on during my first life-time, thanks to being chosen by Demeter to be brought into the Order of Amazons. I had still been a relative child when I learned that my world was really a ship and was shown my first, terrifyingly beautiful glimpse of the endless depths of Earth's strange blue sky. By the time we had finally reached Earth, I walked off the *Tartarus* and didn't look back. I was done with walls, with cages. Or so I had thought.

But living under Demeter's rule was a cage of its own, and I hadn't known true freedom until the day I defied her. Until the day I died to save our people. And now the Tsakali were coming to Earth once more, a swarm of destruction driven by a warped sense of revenge burning in their hearts.

I sighed and bowed my head. "We're not going to be able to do anything to prevent the Tsakali invasion, are we?" I could feel myself slowly, reluctantly accepting the truth.

A soft, bitter laugh escaped from Hades' chest, and his stare wandered back to the gephyra. "No, I don't believe so."

I frowned, still hoping there was a way to save Earth. To save all those people. In a sense, they were my people, too. "But what if Henry was onto something—about the Tsakali's hatred of our people?" I said, rushing to say more before Hades could dismiss the idea outright. "If we leave and destroy all traces of Olympians and chaos stones from the planet, and all that the Tsakali find when they arrive are humans and their relatively primitive technology, maybe the Tsakali will just move on?"

Hades' shoulders slumped, and he shook his head. "I wish it were that simple. But the truth of the matter is that humans have too much of us in them."

I looked at Hades, my brows bunching together.

"As we tweaked the humans' genetic code over the years to make them compatible hosts for Olympian consciousnesses," he explained, "we inserted pieces of our own DNA. Too many pieces, I'm afraid. The Tsakali will detect our touch. They will know we were here, and they will hold this world hostage until they get what they want . . . or until they destroy it out of misguided retribution."

I faced Hades, leaning my hip against the railing and crossing my arms over my chest. "So, humanity can either cooperate with the Tsakali—and doom the universe—or fight them and die." Of course, I knew we couldn't *let* them cooperate. "Excluding those lucky few we evacuate aboard this ship."

Hades took a moment to respond. "Pretty much," he said grimly.

I pursed my lips, quirking them to the side as possibilities danced through my mind. "What if there's another option?"

Hades looked at me sidelong, his eyebrows raised.

"How many souls can the *Elysium* hold?" I asked. I wasn't talking about people with physical bodies, but disembodied consciousnesses, like those still contained within the Vault of Souls in the Omega site.

Hades narrowed his eyes thoughtfully. "A little over two billion," he said, then added, "Minus the spots taken by the millions of Olympians already residing here and those we'll be adding." The ship hadn't been empty when we had found it. Far from it, in fact. It looked like the people who had abandoned the frozen settlement mid-construction had all uploaded their consciousnesses into the *Elysium's* supersized Vault of Souls, though we still didn't know *why* they had fled into the ship.

I nodded to myself. There wouldn't be enough room to fit all of humanity, but there would be space for a good chunk. Far more than we could carry bodily. Enough that humans of Earth could live on, elsewhere, even if their world died.

"If we let the humans share their knowledge of the chaos stones with the Tsakali, then the universe is doomed," I said, thinking out loud. "And if we leave them to fend for themselves, all traces of chaos stones wiped from the planet, then *their world* is doomed. But if we evacuate as many as we can into the Vault of Souls here, aboard this ship, they have a real chance of surviving."

Hades' expression turned thoughtful, considering.

"I think we owe them that much, at least," I said, turning partway as my gaze drifted down to where my mom sat at the navigation terminal. "This war may never have reached them, if not for us."

My mom didn't know about the last resort—unleashing a

weapon that would turn Earth into something resembling the first colony we had visited. None of the humans aboard the *Elysium* knew, and I was terrified of telling them what we might have to do. At least this way, I might be able to offer something of a consolation prize—far greater than what we had thought was possible.

I could feel Hades' stare on the side of my face. "It won't be easy, convincing the humans to abandon everything they know to come with us."

I blew out a breath, relieved that he was open to the idea.

"To many, they will be unable to see existence in the Vault of Souls as anything other than death," he continued. "I don't know that many will choose to come. Unless you mean to take them unwillingly . . ."

I shook my head, still looking down on my mom. "No, we give them a choice . . ." I glanced at Hades, the corner of my mouth tensing. "We just don't tell them their bodies won't be coming with their minds when they board the ship."

After all, we had Fiona *and* all of Hades' techies—how hard could it really be to create a new world for humanity within the *Elysium's* Vault of Souls? A virtual world, as real as the one they had left behind, where they would be safe while we searched for a new place to call home. Or better yet, while we searched for a way to defeat the Tsakali, once and for all. They wouldn't need to know the truth until it was all over and done with.

And more importantly, they would survive.

▭

Thanks for reading! You've reached the end of Dreams of the Damned, *but the story continues in* Song of the Soulless.

Go to authorlindseysparks.com/sacrifice to grab a free copy of <u>Sacrifice of the Sinners</u>, *the Atlantis Legacy prequel.*

MORE BOOK BY LINDSEY SPARKS

ECHO TRILOGY

Echo in Time

Resonance

Time Anomaly

Dissonance

Ricochet Through Time

KAT DUBOIS CHRONICLES

Ink Witch

Outcast

Underground

Soul Eater

Judgement

Afterlife

ATLANTIS LEGACY

Sacrifice of the Sinners

Legacy of the Lost

Fate of the Fallen

Dreams of the Damned

Song of the Soulless

Blood of the Broken

Rise of the Revenants

<u>ALLWORLD ONLINE</u>

<u>AO: Pride & Prejudice</u>

<u>AO: The Wonderful Wizard of Oz</u>

<u>Vertigo</u>

THE ENDING SERIES

<u>The Ending Beginnings: Omnibus Edition</u>

<u>After The Ending</u>

<u>Into The Fire</u>

<u>Out Of The Ashes</u>

<u>Before The Dawn</u>

<u>World Before</u>

THE ENDING LEGACY

<u>World After</u>

For more information on Lindsey and her books:

<u>www.authorlindseysparks.com</u>

Join Lindsey's mailing list to stay up to date on releases

AND to get a FREE copy of *Sacrifice of the Sinners*.

<u>www.authorlindseysparks.com/sacrifice</u>

To read Lindsey's books as she writes them, check her out on Patreon:

<u>https://www.patreon.com/lindseysparks</u>

Lindsey Sparks is a bestselling Science Fiction and Fantasy author who lives her life with one foot in a book—so long as that book transports her to a magical world or bends the rules of science. Her novels, from Post-apocalyptic to Time Travel Romance, always offer up a hearty dose of unreality,  along with plenty of history, mystery, adventure, and romance.

When she's not working on her next novel, Lindsey spends her time hanging out with her two little boys, working in her garden, or playing board games with her husband. She lives in the Pacific Northwest with her family and their small pack of cats and dogs.

www.authorlindseysparks.com

Facebook: www.facebook.com/authorlindseysparks
Facebook Reader Group: www.facebook.com/groups/lovelyreaders
Instagram: @authorlindseysparks
Pinterest: www.pinterest.com/authorlindseysparks
Newsletter: www.authorlindseysparks.com/join-newsletter
Patreon: www.patreon.com/lindseysparks

www.ingramcontent.com/pod-product-compliance
Lightning Source LLC
Chambersburg PA
CBHW050850190726

48286CB00007B/2318